The Oranging of America

Max Apple

The Oranging of America

and other stories

Grossman Publishers

A DIVISION OF THE VIKING PRESS
NEW YORK

Copyright © Max Apple, 1974, 1975, 1976
All rights reserved
First published in 1976 by Grossman Publishers
625 Madison Avenue, New York, N.Y. 10022
Published simultaneously in Canada by
The Macmillan Company of Canada Limited
Second printing February 1977
Printed in the United States of America

Library of Congress Cataloging in Publication Data

Apple, Max.
  The oranging of America, and other stories.

  Contents: Patty-Cake, Patty-Cake.—Inside Norman Mailer.—Selling
out. [etc.]
  I. Title.
PZ4.A6476or [PS3551.P56] 813'.5'4 76-23436
ISBN 0-670-52801-3

Some of these stories originally appeared in *The American Review,
Esquire, The Georgia Review, New and Experimental Literature,
The Ohio Review*

In memory of my father
and my grandmother

and for Ted Solotaroff

Contents

The Oranging
of America

I

From the outside it looked like any ordinary 1964 Cadillac limousine. In the expensive space between the driver and passengers, where some installed bars or even bathrooms, Mr. Howard Johnson kept a tidy ice-cream freezer in which there were always at least eighteen flavors on hand, though Mr. Johnson ate only vanilla. The freezer's power came from the battery with an independent auxiliary generator as a back-up system. Although now Howard Johnson means primarily motels, Millie, Mr. HJ, and Otis Brighton, the chauffeur, had not forgotten that ice cream was the cornerstone of their empire. Some of the important tasting was still done in the car. Mr. HJ might have reports in his pocket from sales executives and marketing analysts, from home economists and chemists, but not until Mr. Johnson reached over the lowered Plexiglas to spoon a taste or two into the expert waiting mouth of Otis Brighton did he make any final flavor decision. He might go ahead with butterfly shrimp, with candy kisses, and with packaged chocolate-chip cookies on the opinion of the specialists, but in ice cream he trusted only Otis. From the back seat Howard Johnson would keep his eye on the rearview mirror, where the reflection of pleasure or disgust showed itself in the dark eyes of Otis Brighton no matter what the driving conditions. He could be stalled in a commuter rush with the engine overheating and a dripping oil pan, and still a taste of the right kind never went unappreciated.

When Otis finally said, "Mr. Howard, that shore is sumpin, that one is um-hum. That is it, my man, that is it." Then and not until then did Mr. HJ finally decide to go ahead with something like banana-fudge-ripple royale.

Mildred rarely tasted and Mr. HJ was addicted to one scoop of vanilla every afternoon at three, eaten from his aluminum dish with a disposable plastic spoon. The duties of Otis, Millie, and Mr. Johnson were so divided that they rarely infringed upon one another in the car, which was their office. Neither Mr. HJ nor Millie knew how to drive, Millie and Otis understood little of financing and leasing, and Mr. HJ left the compiling of the "Traveling Reports" and "The Howard Johnson Newsletter" strictly to the literary style of his longtime associate, Miss Mildred Bryce. It was an ideal division of labor, which, in one form or another, had been in continuous operation for well over a quarter of a century.

While Otis listened to the radio behind his soundproof Plexiglas, while Millie in her small, neat hand compiled data for the newsletter, Mr. HJ liked to lean back into the spongy leather seat looking through his specially tinted windshield at the fleeting land. Occasionally, lulled by the hum of the freezer, he might doze off, his large pink head lolling toward the shoulder of his blue suit, but there was not too much that Mr. Johnson missed, even in advanced age.

Along with Millie he planned their continuous itinerary as they traveled. Mildred would tape a large green relief map of the United States to the Plexiglas separating them from Otis. The mountains on the map were light brown and seemed to melt toward the valleys like the crust of a fresh apple pie settling into cinnamon surroundings. The existing HJ houses (Millie called the restaurants and motels houses) were marked by orange dots, while projected future sites bore white dots. The deep green map with its brown mountains and colorful dots seemed much more alive than the miles that twinkled past Mr. Johnson's gaze, and nothing gave the ice-cream king greater pleasure than watching Mildred with her fine touch, and using the original crayon, turn an empty white dot into an orange fulfillment.

"It's like a seed grown into a tree, Millie," Mr. HJ liked to say at such moments when he contemplated the map and saw that it was good.

They had started traveling together in 1925: Mildred, then a secretary to Mr. Johnson, a young man with two restaurants and a dream of hospitality, and Otis, a twenty-year-old busboy and former driver of a Louisiana mule. When Mildred graduated from college, her father, a Michigan doctor who kept his money in a blue steel box under the examining table, encouraged her to try the big city. He sent her a monthly allowance. In those early days she always had more than Mr. Johnson, who paid her $16.50 a week and meals. In the first decade they traveled only on weekends, but every year since 1936 they had spent at least six months on the road, and it might have gone on much longer if Mildred's pain and the trouble in New York with Howard Jr. had not come so close together.

They were all stoical at the Los Angeles International Airport. Otis waited at the car for what might be his last job while Miss Bryce and Mr. Johnson traveled toward the New York plane along a silent moving floor. Millie stood beside Howard while they passed a mural of a Mexican landscape and some Christmas drawings by fourth graders from Watts. For forty years they had been together in spite of Sonny and the others, but at this most recent appeal from New York Millie urged him to go back. Sonny had cabled, "My God, Dad, you're sixty-nine years old, haven't you been a gypsy long enough? Board meeting December third with or without you. Policy changes imminent."

Normally, they ignored Sonny's cables, but this time Millie wanted him to go, wanted to be alone with the pain that had recently come to her. She had left Howard holding the new canvas suitcase in which she had packed her three notebooks of regional reports along with his aluminum dish, and in a moment of real despair she had even packed the orange crayon. When Howard boarded Flight 965 he looked old to Millie. His feet dragged in the wing-tipped shoes, the hand she shook was moist, the lip felt dry, and as he passed from her sight down the entry ramp Mildred Bryce felt a fresh new ache that sent her hobbling toward the car. Otis had unplugged the freezer, and the silence caused by the missing hum was as intense to Millie as her abdominal pain.

It had come quite suddenly in Albuquerque, New Mexico, at the grand opening of a 210-unit house. She did not make a fuss. Mildred Bryce had never caused trouble to anyone, except perhaps to Mrs. HJ. Millie's quick precise actions, angular face, and thin body made her seem birdlike, especially next to Mr. HJ, six three with splendid white hair accenting his dark blue gabardine suits. Howard was slow and sure. He could sit in the same position for hours while Millie fidgeted on the seat, wrote memos, and filed reports in the small gray cabinet that sat in front of her and parallel to the ice-cream freezer. Her health had always been good, so at first she tried to ignore the pain. It was gas: it was perhaps the New Mexico water or the cooking oil in the fish dinner. But she could not convince away the pain. It stayed like a match burning around her belly, etching itself into her as the round HJ emblem was so symmetrically embroidered into the bedspread, which she had kicked off in the flush that accompanied the pain. She felt as if her sweat would engulf the foam mattress and crisp percale sheet. Finally, Millie brought up her knees and made a ball of herself as if being as small as possible might make her misery disappear. It worked for everything except the pain. The little circle of hot torment was all that remained of her, and when finally at sometime in the early morning it left, it occurred to her that perhaps she had struggled with a demon and been suddenly relieved by the coming of daylight. She stepped lightly into the bathroom and before a full-length mirror (new in HJ motels exclusively) saw herself whole and unmarked, but sign enough to Mildred was her smell, damp and musty, sign enough that something had begun and that something else would therefore necessarily end.

II

Before she had the report from her doctor, Howard Jr.'s message had given her the excuse she needed. There was no reason why

Millie could not tell Howard she was sick, but telling him would be admitting too much to herself. Along with Howard Johnson Millie had grown rich beyond dreams. Her inheritance, the $100,000 from her father's steel box in 1939, went directly to Mr. Johnson, who desperately needed it, and the results of that investment brought Millie enough capital to employ two people at the Chase Manhattan with the management of her finances. With money beyond the hope of use, she had vacationed all over the world and spent some time in the company of celebrities, but the reality of her life, like his, was in the back seat of the limousine, waiting for that point at which the needs of the automobile and the human body met the undeviating purpose of the highway and momentarily conquered it.

Her life was measured in rest stops. She, Howard, and Otis had found them out before they existed. They knew the places to stop between Buffalo and Albany, Chicago and Milwaukee, Toledo and Columbus, Des Moines and Minneapolis, they knew through their own bodies, measured in hunger and discomfort in the '30s and '40s when they would stop at remote places to buy land and borrow money, sensing in themselves the hunger that would one day be upon the place. People were wary and Howard had trouble borrowing (her $100,000 had perhaps been the key) but invariably he was right. Howard knew the land, Mildred thought, the way the Indians must have known it. There were even spots along the way where the earth itself seemed to make men stop. Howard had a sixth sense that would sometimes lead them from the main roads to, say, a dark green field in Iowa or Kansas. Howard, who might have seemed asleep, would rap with his knuckles on the Plexiglas, causing the knowing Otis to bring the car to such a quick stop that Millie almost flew into her filing cabinet. And before the emergency brake had settled into its final prong, Howard Johnson was into the field and after the scent. While Millie and Otis waited, he would walk it out slowly. Sometimes he would sit down, disappearing in a field of long and tangled weeds, or he might find a large smooth rock to sit on while he felt some secret vibration from the place. Turning his back to Millie, he would mark the spot with his urine or

break some of the clayey earth in his strong pink hands, sifting
it like flour for a delicate recipe. She had actually seen him chew
the grass, getting down on all fours like an animal and biting
the tops without pulling the entire blade from the soil. At
times he ran in a slow jog as far as his aging legs would carry
him. Whenever he slipped out of sight behind the uneven terrain,
Millie felt him in danger, felt that something alien might be
there to resist the civilizing instinct of Howard Johnson. Once
when Howard had been out of sight for more than an hour and
did not respond to their frantic calls, Millie sent Otis into the
field and in desperation flagged a passing car.

"Howard Johnson is lost in that field," she told the surprised
driver. "He went in to look for a new location and we can't find
him now."

"The restaurant Howard Johnson?" the man asked.

"Yes. Help us please."

The man drove off, leaving Millie to taste in his exhaust fumes
the barbarism of an ungrateful public. Otis found Howard asleep
in a field of light blue wild flowers. He had collapsed from the
exertion of his run. Millie brought water to him, and when he
felt better, right there in the field, he ate his scoop of vanilla on
the very spot where three years later they opened the first fully
air-conditioned motel in the world. When she stopped to think
about it, Millie knew they were more than businessmen, they
were pioneers.

And once, while on her own, she had the feeling too. In 1951
when she visited the Holy Land there was an inkling of what
Howard must have felt all the time. It happened without any
warning on a bus crowded with tourists and resident Arabs on
their way to the Dead Sea. Past ancient Sodom the bus creaked
and bumped, down, down, toward the lowest point on earth,
when suddenly in the midst of the crowd and her stomach queasy
with the motion of the bus, Mildred Bryce experienced an over-
whelming calm. A light brown patch of earth surrounded by a
few pale desert rocks overwhelmed her perception, seemed closer
to her than the Arab lady in the black flowered dress pushing

her basket against Millie at that very moment. She wanted to stop the bus. Had she been near the door she might have actually jumped, so strong was her sensitivity to that barren spot in the endless desert. Her whole body ached for it as if in unison, bone by bone. Her limbs tingled, her breath came in short gasps, the sky rolled out of the bus windows and obliterated her view. The Arab lady spat on the floor and moved a suspicious eye over a squirming Mildred.

When the bus stopped at the Dead Sea, the Arabs and tourists rushed to the soupy brine clutching damaged limbs, while Millie pressed twenty dollars American into the dirty palm of a cab-driver who took her back to the very place where the music of her body began once more as sweetly as the first time. While the incredulous driver waited, Millie walked about the place wishing Howard were there to understand her new understanding of his kind of process. There was nothing there, absolutely nothing but pure bliss. The sun beat her like a wish, the air was hot and stale as a Viennese bathhouse, and yet Mildred felt peace and rest there, and as her cab bill mounted she actually did rest in the miserable barren desert of an altogether unsatisfactory land. When the driver, wiping the sweat from his neck, asked, "Meesez . . . pleeze. Why American woman wants Old Jericho in such kind of heat?" When he said "Jericho," she understood that this was a place where men had always stopped. In dim antiquity Jacob had perhaps watered a flock here, and not far away Lot's wife paused to scan for the last time the city of her youth. Perhaps Mildred now stood where Abraham had been visited by a vision and, making a rock his pillow, had first put the ease into the earth. Whatever it was, Millie knew from her own experience that rest was created here by historical precedent. She tried to buy that piece of land, going as far as King Hussein's secretary of the interior. She imagined a Palestinian HJ with an orange roof angling toward Sodom, a seafood restaurant, and an oasis of fresh fruit. But the land was in dispute between Israel and Jordan, and even King Hussein, who expressed admiration for Howard Johnson, could not sell to Millie the place of her comfort.

That was her single visionary moment, but sharing them with Howard was almost as good. And to end all this, to finally stay in her eighteenth-floor Santa Monica penthouse, where the Pacific dived into California, this seemed to Mildred a paltry conclusion to an adventurous life. Her doctor said it was not so serious, she had a bleeding ulcer and must watch her diet. The prognosis was, in fact, excellent. But Mildred, fifty-six and alone in California, found the doctor less comforting than most of the rest stops she had experienced.

III

California, right after the Second War, was hardly a civilized place for travelers. Millie, HJ, and Otis had a twelve-cylinder '47 Lincoln and snaked along five days between Sacramento and Los Angeles. "Comfort, comfort," said HJ as he surveyed the redwood forest and the bubbly surf while it slipped away from Otis, who had rolled his trousers to chase the ocean away during a stop near San Francisco. Howard Johnson was contemplative in California. They had never been in the West before. Their route, always slightly new, was yet bound by Canada, where a person couldn't get a tax break, and roughly by the Mississippi as a western frontier. Their journeys took them up the eastern seaboard and through New England to the early reaches of the Midwest, stopping at the plains of Wisconsin and the cool crisp edge of Chicago where two HJ lodges twinkled at the lake.

One day in 1947 while on the way from Chicago to Cairo, Illinois, HJ looked long at the green relief maps. While Millie kept busy with her filing, HJ loosened the tape and placed the map across his soft round knees. The map jiggled and sagged, the Mid- and Southwest hanging between his legs. When Mildred finally noticed that look, he had been staring at the map for perhaps fifteen minutes, brooding over it, and Millie knew something was in the air.

HJ looked at that map the way some people looked down from an airplane trying to pick out the familiar from the colorful mass receding beneath them. Howard Johnson's eye flew over the land—over the Tetons, over the Sierra Nevada, over the long thin gouge of the Canyon flew his gaze—charting his course by rest stops the way an antique mariner might have gazed at the stars.

"Millie," he said just north of Carbondale, "Millie..." He looked toward her, saw her fingers engaged and her thumbs circling each other in anticipation. He looked at Millie and saw that she saw what he saw. "Millie"—HJ raised his right arm and its shadow spread across the continent like a prophecy— "Millie, what if we turn right at Cairo and go that way?" California, already peeling on the green map, balanced on HJ's left knee like a happy child.

Twenty years later Mildred settled in her eighteenth-floor apartment in the building owned by Lawrence Welk. Howard was in New York, Otis and the car waited in Arizona. The pain did not return as powerfully as it had appeared that night in Albuquerque, but it hurt with dull regularity and an occasional streak of dark blood from her bowels kept her mind on it even on painless days.

Directly beneath her gaze were the organized activities of the golden-age groups, tiny figures playing bridge or shuffleboard or looking out at the water from their benches as she sat on her sofa and looked out at them and the fluffy ocean. Mildred did not regret family life. The HJ houses were her offspring. She had watched them blossom from the rough youngsters of the '40s with steam heat and even occasional kitchenettes into cool mature adults with king-sized beds, color TVs, and room service. Her late years were spent comfortably in the modern houses just as one might enjoy in age the benefits of a child's prosperity. She regretted only that it was probably over.

But she did not give up completely until she received a personal letter one day telling her that she was eligible for burial insurance until age eighty. A $1000 policy would guarantee a complete and dignified service. Millie crumpled the advertisement, but a few hours later called her Los Angeles lawyer. As she suspected, there were no plans, but as the executor of the estate he would assume full responsibility, subject of course to her approval.

"I'll do it myself," Millie had said, but she could not bring herself to do it. The idea was too alien. In more than forty years Mildred had not gone a day without a shower and change of underclothing. Everything about her suggested order and precision. Her fingernails were shaped so that the soft meat of the tips could stroke a typewriter without damaging the apex of a nail, her arch slid over a 6B shoe like an egg in a shell, and never in her adult life did Mildred recall having vomited. It did not seem right to suddenly let all this sink into the dark earth of Forest Lawn because some organ or other developed a hole as big as a nickel. It was not right and she wouldn't do it. Her first idea was to stay in the apartment, to write it into the lease if necessary. She had the lawyer make an appointment for her with Mr. Welk's management firm, but canceled it the day before. "They will just think I'm crazy," she said aloud to herself, "and they'll bury me anyway."

She thought of cryonics while reading a biography of William Chesebrough, the man who invented petroleum jelly. Howard had known him and often mentioned that his own daily ritual of the scoop of vanilla was like old Chesebrough's two teaspoons of Vaseline every day. Chesebrough lived to be ninety. In the biography it said that after taking the daily dose of Vaseline, he drank three cups of green tea to melt everything down, rested for twelve minutes, and then felt fit as a young man, even in his late eighties. When he died they froze his body and Millie had her idea. The Vaseline people kept him in a secret laboratory somewhere near Cleveland and claimed he was in better condition than Lenin, whom the Russians kept hermetically sealed, but at room temperature.

In the phone book she found the Los Angeles Cryonic Society and asked it to send her information. It all seemed very clean. The cost was $200 a year for maintaining the cold. She sent the pamphlet to her lawyer to be sure that the society was legitimate. It wasn't much money, but, still, if they were charlatans, she didn't want them to take advantage of her even if she would never know about it. They were aboveboard, the lawyer said. "The interest on a ten-thousand-dollar trust fund would pay about five hundred a year," the lawyer said, "and they only charge two hundred dollars. Still, who knows what the cost might be in say two hundred years?" To be extra safe, they put $25,000 in trust for eternal maintenance, to be eternally overseen by Longstreet, Williams, and their eternal heirs. When it was arranged, Mildred felt better than she had in weeks.

IV

Four months to the day after she had left Howard at the Los Angeles International Airport, he returned for Mildred without the slightest warning. She was in her housecoat and had not even washed the night cream from her cheeks when she saw through the viewing space in her door the familiar long pink jowls, even longer in the distorted glass.

"Howard," she gasped, fumbling with the door, and in an instant he was there picking her up as he might a child or an ice-cream cone while her tears fell like dandruff on his blue suit. While Millie sobbed into his soft padded shoulder, HJ told her the good news. "I'm chairman emeritus of the board now. That means no more New York responsibilities. They still have to listen to me because we hold the majority of the stock, but Howard Junior and Keyes will take care of the business. Our main job is new home-owned franchises. And, Millie, guess where we're going first?"

So overcome was Mildred that she could not hold back her sobs even to guess. Howard Johnson put her down, beaming pleasure through his old bright eyes. "Florida," HJ said, then slowly repeated it, "Flor-idda, and guess what we're going to do?"

"Howard," Millie said, swiping at her tears with the filmy lace cuffs of her dressing gown, "I'm so surprised I don't know what to say. You could tell me we're going to the moon and I'd believe you. Just seeing you again has brought back all my hope." They came out of the hallway and sat on the sofa that looked out over

the Pacific. HJ, all pink, kept his hands on his knees like paper-
weights.

"Millie, you're almost right. I can't fool you about anything
and never could. We're going down near where they launch the
rockets from. I've heard . . ." HJ leaned toward the kitchen as if
to check for spies. He looked at the stainless-steel-and-glass table,
at the built-in avocado appliances, then leaned his large moist
lips toward Mildred's ear. "Walt Disney is planning right this
minute a new Disneyland down there. They're trying to keep it
a secret, but his brother Roy bought options on thousands of
acres. We're going down to buy as much as we can as close in
as we can." Howard sparkled. "Millie, don't you see, it's a sure
thing."

After her emotional outburst at seeing Howard again, a calmer
Millie felt a slight twitch in her upper stomach and in the midst
of her joy was reminded of another sure thing.

They would be a few weeks in Los Angeles anyway. Howard
wanted to thoroughly scout out the existing Disneyland, so Millie
had some time to think it out. She could go, as her heart directed
her, with HJ to Florida and points beyond. She could take the
future as it happened like a Disneyland ride or she could listen
to the dismal eloquence of her ulcer and try to make the best
arrangements she could. Howard and Otis would take care of her
to the end, there were no doubts about that, and the end would
be the end. But if she stayed in this apartment, sure of the arrangements for later, she would miss whatever might still be left
before the end. Mildred wished there were some clergyman she
could consult, but she had never attended a church and believed
in no religious doctrine. Her father had been a firm atheist to
the very moment of his office suicide, and she remained a passive
nonbeliever. Her theology was the order of her own life. Millie
had never deceived herself; in spite of her riches all she truly
owned was her life, a pocket of habits in the burning universe.
But the habits were careful and clean and they were best represented in the body that was she. Freezing her remains was the
closest image she could conjure of eternal life. It might not be
eternal and it surely would not be life, but that damp, musty

feel, that odor she smelled on herself after the pain, that could be avoided, and who knew what else might be saved from the void for a small initial investment and $200 a year. And if you did not believe in a soul, was there not every reason to preserve a body?

Mrs. Albert of the Cryonic Society welcomed Mildred to a tour of the premises. "See it while you can," she cheerfully told the group (Millie, two men, and a boy with notebook and Polaroid camera). Mrs. Albert, a big woman perhaps in her mid-sixties, carried a face heavy in flesh. Perhaps once the skin had been tight around her long chin and pointed cheekbones, but having lost its spring, the skin merely hung at her neck like a patient animal waiting for the rest of her to join in the decline. From the way she took the concrete stairs down to the vault, it looked as if the wait would be long. "I'm not ready for the freezer yet. I tell every group I take down here, it's gonna be a long time until they get me." Millie believed her. "I may not be the world's smartest cookie"—Mrs. Albert looked directly at Millie—"but a bird in the hand is the only bird I know, huh? That's why when it does come . . . Mrs. A is going to be right here in this facility, and you better believe it. Now, Mr. King on your left"—she pointed to a capsule that looked like a large bullet to Millie— "Mr. King is the gentleman who took me on my first tour, cancer finally but had everything perfectly ready and I would say he was in prime cooling state within seconds and I believe that if they ever cure cancer, and you know they will the way they do most everything nowadays, old Mr. King may be back yet. If anyone got down to low-enough temperature immediately it would be Mr. King." Mildred saw the boy write "Return of the King" in his notebook. "Over here is Mr. and Mizz Winkleman, married sixty years, and went off within a month of each other, a lovely, lovely couple."

While Mrs. Albert continued her necrology and posed for a photo beside the Winklemans, Millie took careful note of the neon-lit room filled with bulletlike capsules. She watched the cool breaths of the group gather like flowers on the steel and vanish without dimming the bright surface. The capsules stood in straight lines with ample walking space between them. To Mrs. Albert they were friends, to Millie it seemed as if she were in a furniture store of the Scandinavian type where elegance is suggested by the absence of material, where straight lines of steel, wood, and glass indicate that relaxation too requires some taste and is not an indifferent sprawl across any soft object that happens to be nearby.

Cemeteries always bothered Millie, but here she felt none of the dread she had expected. She averted her eyes from the cluttered graveyards they always used to pass at the tips of cities in the early days. Fortunately, the superhighways twisted traffic into the city and away from those desolate marking places where used-car lots and the names of famous hotels inscribed on barns often neighbored the dead. Howard had once commented that never in all his experience did he have an intuition of a good location near a cemetery. You could put a lot of things there, you could put up a bowling alley, or maybe even a theater, but never a motel, and Millie knew he was right. He knew where to put his houses but it was Millie who knew how. From that first orange roof angling toward the east, the HJ design and the idea had been Millie's. She had not invented the motel, she had changed it from a place where you had to be to a place where you wanted to be. Perhaps, she thought, the Cryonic Society was trying to do the same for cemeteries.

When she and Howard had started their travels, the old motel courts huddled like so many dark graves around the stone marking of the highway. And what traveler coming into one of those dingy cabins could watch the watery rust dripping from his faucet without thinking of everything he was missing by being a traveler . . . his two-stall garage, his wife small in the half-empty bed, his children with hair the color of that rust. Under the orange Howard Johnson roof all this changed. For about the same price you were redeemed from the road. Headlights did not dazzle you on the foam mattress and percale sheets, your sanitized glasses and toilet appliances sparkled like the mirror behind them. The room was not just there, it awaited you, courted your pleasure, sat like a young bride outside the walls of the city wanting only to please you, you only you on the smoothly pressed sheets, your friend, your one-night destiny.

As if it were yesterday, Millie recalled right there in the cryonic vault the moment when she had first thought the thought that made Howard Johnson Howard Johnson's. And when she told Howard her decision that evening after cooking a cheese soufflé and risking a taste of wine, it was that memory she invoked for both of them, the memory of a cool autumn day in the '30s when a break in their schedule found Millie with a free afternoon in New Hampshire, an afternoon she had spent at the farm of a man who had once been her teacher and remembered her after ten years. Otis drove her out to Robert Frost's farm, where the poet made for her a lunch of scrambled eggs and 7 Up. Millie and Robert Frost talked mostly about the farm, about the cold winter he was expecting and the autumn apples they picked from the trees. He was not so famous then, his hair was only streaked with gray as Howard's was, and she told the poet about what she and Howard were doing, about what she felt about being on the road in America, and Robert Frost said he hadn't been that much but she sounded like she knew and he believed she might be able to accomplish something. He did not remember the poem she wrote in his class but that didn't matter.

"Do you remember, Howard, how I introduced you to him? Mr. Frost, this is Mr. Johnson. I can still see the two of you shaking hands there beside the car. I've always been proud that I introduced you to one another." Howard Johnson nodded his head at the memory, seemed as nostalgic as Millie while he sat in her apartment learning why she would not go to Florida to help bring Howard Johnson's to the new Disneyland.

"And after we left his farm, Howard, remember? Otis took the car in for servicing and left us with some sandwiches on the top of a hill overlooking a town, I don't even remember which one, maybe we never knew the name of it. And we stayed on that hilltop while the sun began to set in New Hampshire. I felt so full of poetry and"—she looked at Howard—"of love, Howard, only about an hour's drive from Robert Frost's farmhouse. Maybe it was just the way we felt then, but I think the sun set differently that night, filtering through the clouds like a big paintbrush making the top of the town all orange. And suddenly I thought what if the tops of our houses were that kind of orange, what a world it would be, Howard, and my God, that orange stayed until the last drop of light was left in it. I didn't feel the cold up there even though it took Otis so long to get back to us. The feeling we had about that orange, Howard, that was ours and that's what I've tried to bring to every house, the way we felt that night. Oh, it makes me sick to think of Colonel Sanders, and Big Boy, and Holiday Inn, and Best Western . . ."

"It's all right, Millie, it's all right." Howard patted her heaving back. Now that he knew about her ulcer and why she wanted to stay behind, the mind that had conjured butterfly shrimp and twenty-eight flavors set himself a new project. He contemplated Millie sobbing in his lap the way he contemplated prime acreage. There was so little of her, less than one hundred pounds, yet without her Howard Johnson felt himself no match for the wily Disneys gathering near the moonport.

He left her in all her sad resignation that evening, left her thinking she had to give up what remained here to be sure of the proper freezing. But Howard Johnson had other ideas. He did not cancel the advance reservations made for Mildred Bryce along the route to Florida, nor did he remove her filing cabinet from the limousine. The man who hosted a nation and already kept one freezer in his car merely ordered another, this one designed according to cryonic specifications and presented to Mildred housed in a twelve-foot orange U-Haul trailer connected to the rear bumper of the limousine.

"Everything's here," he told the astonished Millie, who thought Howard had left the week before, "everything is here and you'll never have to be more than seconds away from it. It's exactly like a refrigerated truck." Howard Johnson opened the rear door of the U-Haul as proudly as he had ever dedicated a motel. Millie's steel capsule shone within, surrounded by an array of chemicals stored on heavily padded rubber shelves. The California sun was on her back, but her cold breath hovered visibly within the

U-Haul. No tears came to Mildred now; she felt relief much as she had felt it that afternoon near ancient Jericho. On Santa Monica Boulevard, in front of Lawrence Welk's apartment building, Mildred Bryce confronted her immortality, a gift from the ice-cream king, another companion for the remainder of her travels. Howard Johnson had turned away, looking toward the ocean. To his blue back and patriarchal white hairs, Mildred said, "Howard, you can do anything," and closing the doors of the U-Haul, she joined the host of the highways, a man with two portable freezers, ready now for the challenge of Disney World.

Selling Out

I

When he was thirty, my father, a careful man, bought a "piece of the Rock," a twenty-thousand dollar chunk to be exact. At thirty-eight, in good health and during the Korean War, he doubled it. At forty-six with a slightly elevated BP (155/94) they let him buy fifteen thousand additional with a ten-percent premium hike. At fifty he beat the actuarial tables. We thought it was only an upset stomach. He dropped two Alka Seltzers in a half glass of water and died before they melted. After funeral expenses I was left with $53,000, which the Prudential man wanted me to leave in on a million-dollar policy on myself.

"I'll take the fifty-three," I said.

My father's cousin, H.B., a broker, said, "For safety's sake let's put it in a fund. There you're protected. Who knows what can happen with an individual stock? And far be it from me to take upon myself the responsibility of a discretionary account for my orphaned cousin. However, if you'd like . . ."

"Buy the fund," I said.

The commissions came out to a little over three thousand; that left between forty-nine and fifty thousand. It was in 1965.

I put it all out of mind, worked in a bookstore, and went to community college at night. The fund reinvested the dividends and capital gains. In the hot market of early 1968 I had on one particular day, April 7, $187,000 in the fund. The next April 7 it was down to $81,000. I always check on April 7 because it's the day Dad died. Every Christmas when I get a calendar from H.B.'s office, right after I fold out its clever cardboard leg, I circle April 7 and try to buy the *Journal* for the eighth. I called H.B. in 1969 to tell him I was down $106,000 in one year.

"It's the goddamn war," he said. "It's killing the street. And the back-room mess is worse every day. Be glad you're in a fund. The Dow has been underwater for two years. I've got customers calling me saying, 'H.B., I'm dead, should I sell?' Another year like this and I'll be dead too. You can only take so many losses and that's it. Be glad you're in the fund . . . however if you'd like . . ."

"I'll stay in the fund," I said.

In October 1971 I was thirty, not in love, and remembered the fund. A doctor told me I had high blood pressure, ought to lose weight and get more exercise. I had "stroke potential," he said. I thought about it and decided to strike.

I quit the bookstore, shaved my beard, bought a blue gabardine suit, and started reading the *Journal* every day. I also read *Barrons* and the *Dow Theory Forecast*. I answered a Merrill Lynch ad and received a free Standard and Poor's list of all listed stocks in a little gray paperback that looked like a mouse next to my dictionary.

After a month and a half I realized it was futile for me to study the market and made my move anyway. I had planned to wait until April 7, but I was impatient.

In December, my shoes wet with slush, I slid into H.B.'s office wearing my blue suit.

"Please sell the fund," I said.

"What do you mean, sell the fund?"

"Sell it—write out a sell order. How long will the sale take?"

"A minute. It will take a minute, but why sell? Your fund beats the Dow every year. The market is weak."

"How's the back-room mess?"

"Better," he said. "If Nixon takes care of the inflation. You watch us move. Your fund is worth—Mary, add up these figures please." She came through the open door at his side from where

I heard the noise of computers, adding machines, and girl talk. You could smell coffee. In seconds she was back with a slip of white paper for H.B. I noticed her ass when she bent to hand it to him. He looked only at the amount.

"About eighty-seven thousand dollars on today's market."

"Sell it," I said.

"Just like that?"

"Just like that. Are there any commissions?"

"No, you paid them all when you bought in."

"Do I have that money as credit with you right now?"

"As soon as the sale goes through, if you want it."

"Sell it."

"You're sure?"

"I'm sure."

"Mary, sell twelve thousand, four hundred and thirty and a fraction shares of Diversified Fund Ltd." He looked as if large numbers made him sad.

It was 9:07. At 9:11 Mary came back with a confirmation of sale, $87,211.18.

"You can bet one of the fund managers will call me about that sale. It's unusual for them to lose a big chunk all at once. Most people, you know, take it as monthly income. They have faith in the future of the economy."

"I'm going out in the lobby to watch the tape," I said, "and I'm going to start trading against that eighty-seven thousand."

"Trading what? Talk to me a little. How many cousins do I have? You could blow it in an afternoon, everything." Now there were tears in his eyes. I did not doubt his sincerity.

"I might," I said, walking into the lobby where the prices streamed under the ceiling in electric orange. He followed me from his office, and Mary, when I looked back, was peeking from out the back room, leaning way over on one leg.

I sat down in the front row on a padded theater chair. It was like watching a dull French movie. I had a pad and pencil and knew some of the ticker symbols from studying the Standard and Poor's booklet. The first one I recognized was Sony Superscope. I have nothing against the Japs. The selling price at 9:15 was 18.

I wanted to buy in round numbers but 5000 shares came to $90,000.

"Buy forty-five hundred Sony Superscope at eighteen."

On the seat next to me H.B. said, "He's lost his mind." He said it as if I wasn't there.

"Listen," I said, "if you don't want the commissions there are plenty of other brokers." I didn't even look at him but kept my eyes on the board. He added up the price of 4500 shares to be sure I had enough to cover, then he told Mary to buy. Then things were dull for maybe forty-five minutes. Sony was not a hot number at that hour. I watched my purchase go across. It took about a tenth of a second, about as long as it had taken my father's upset stomach to become cardiac arrest.

I smoked some filter-tip Kools that one of the other brokers gave me. H.B. went back to his office. I was almost sorry that I had put everything into the first buy. It made waiting dull. Watching for Sony, I practiced my recognition of the other symbols. I knew only about one in ten. I started checking some in the Standard and Poor's book, but I had only checked Kaiser Aluminum (KL) and US Industries (USI) before I saw Sony Superscope go across at 18¾. H.B. came out and slapped me on the back.

"You knew something, eh? So why couldn't you tell a cousin? Did I ever do anything that wasn't in your best interest?" He slapped me across the shoulders. At 11 Sony hit 19¾ and though I wanted to wait for even numbers, I was bored with SOS and sold. I recognized U.S. Steel and Pabst Brewing and bought a thousand of each. There was enough left to pick up 500 of an unlisted chicken-raising conglomerate that the man on the seat behind me had been watching all morning. At noon I was holding the steel, the beer, and the chickens.

"Mary," I said when I noticed her long thighs in a miniskirt under the flashing orange figures, "would you run out and get me a strawberry malt and some french fries from Mr. Quick?"

She hesitated. "We don't usually . . ." Then she must have caught a high sign from someone in the office behind me. "Glad to," she said as I gave her a dollar. She smelled like an Easter egg.

At the noon break I noticed things in the office surrounding me. The chairs were American Seating (AmS), the desks Shaw Walker (ShW), the toilet paper Scott (Sc). On H.B.'s desk was a Ronson pencil sharpener (Rn), a Sheaffer pen (ShP), and, of course, the back room was full of IBM (IBM) and Xerox (X).

I asked Mary if I could see the label at the back of her blouse as she handed me the french fries. She did not quite blush, waited for a sign, got none, bent toward me as I rose to read Koret of California (KC) above her second vertebra.

"Thank you," I said as she slinked toward the computers, glancing back to me the shared secret of size eight.

I surmised that her underwear was nylon (DuPo). Through the tinted safety glass (LOF) of H.B.'s outer office I noticed two consecutive Mercury Montereys (FM).

That afternoon I traded all of the above. A quarter point I figured for commissions, a half point might be a small profit, but I would have the pleasure of watching the accrual of my father's life move across the big board. Measured in tenths of a second, my father and I controlled about two seconds of the American economy. By 2 p.m. H.B. was constantly at my side. One entire girl in the back room was assigned solely to my transactions. She sweated through her Ban Roll-On (BrM) 51½/62. My only loser was the chicken conglomerate, down ¼. By 2:30 I had come back to the $187,000 of April 7, 1968. I put it all into Occidental Petroleum at 2:35 for two reasons: it was volume leader of the day, and the President, Armand Hammer (like the baking soda), was a friend of V. I. Lenin during the revolution. I sold it at 2:58, making an extra $41,000.

When the orange lights stopped circling the room, H.B. hugged me. "I'm crazy, not you," he said. "It will be a week before the back room can straighten out what you did today. You're a rich man now . . . you were before."

"That's capitalism," I said. "Mary," I called to the back room. She arose from her computer, stepped over a small hill of puts and calls. I held my arm out from my body at the elbow. She fit like destiny and moved in.

Vegetable Love

I

Ferguson was never crazy about chicken, but red meat he shoveled up between fork and thick bread and cleaned his mustache with the tip of his tongue.

Annette Grim taught him otherwise. "I never make love to meat eaters," she said; "it adds the smell of the grave to post-coital depression."

They met at Safeway while he examined Jerusalem artichokes, wondering at their shape and aroma. She was on her way to the health-food island and Ferguson's cart blocked the best route. Just as he had decided to buy the artichokes, Annette pushed the cart aside and he turned to capture, full force, the loaded wire cart upon his groin.

"You poor man," Annette said when she heard his groan, and rushed to him as he leaned against the mushrooms. "You poor, poor, man. I once saw someone get poked in the nuts by an umbrella and they had to call an ambulance." They were alone in the vegetable aisle when she put her long fingers under his zipper, giving comfort as nonchalantly as if she were helping a blind man across the street.

"To me the body is a temple. Would you bring a steak to a temple?"

Later he reminded her that in the original temple they did slaughter animals, smoke the entrails, and did eat the flesh thereof.

"Paganism," said Annette Grim, but by then she had converted him almost beyond argument.

II

His pain blossomed into love. For him she cooked that day a stew of the Jerusalem artichokes, sweet potatoes, turnips, and carrots. Afterward they drank the broth blended with mint leaves, and Ferguson stayed with Annette, gratified by her flesh, but so hungry that at three a.m. he crept from bed and tried to find enough food to sustain him through the night. In her refrigerator she had only brewer's yeast, a coconut, and sprouted mung beans in a baggy thick with mold. In her cupboard were fresh spices from Oregon, a record player, dry mung beans, rolled oats, defatted wheat germ, two rows of empty glass bottles, and a color poster of a bowl of yogurt. Not even bread, he thought, as he slouched toward the bedroom, longing for a McDonald's.

In the first month of their relationship, Ferguson lost fourteen pounds. This was a blessing, since most of it was excess. His clothes, which had been tight, now fit him as they had in 1971 when he weighed one hundred eighty. A sign on her living-room wall reminded him, "The more flesh, the more worms." Yet, rarely from Annette herself did Ferguson hear any direct criticism of his eating habits or his one hundred eighty pounds née one hundred ninety-four. While he marveled at her, his own appetite shrank and his endurance increased. Annette could eat a cup of yogurt and a banana and manage the night in either innocent sleep or full passion without a hunger pain. She was five feet five and weighed an unvarying one hundred and eight pounds. She was eighty percent protein and water. She used no deodorants, nor did she shave her legs or underarms or cut her hair. She brushed her teeth with baking soda and a one-thousand-sheet roll of toilet tissue could last her a month. She hadn't had a cold since the day after Nixon announced the bombing of Hanoi and Haiphong.

Next to her, Ferguson felt like an ineffective cancer. Full of dead meats, artificial flavors, and additives, he attached himself to her, but so whole was her purity that his soft and weak one hundred eighty pounds of pulsating tissue limped back to itself without touching what she called "the center of my consciousness." This she had worked out herself, a sort of Cartesian pineal gland that existed within her right rib cage. "This is its place, my body's soul lives here. This is not the spirit or soul that maybe doesn't exist. This is a real one. You can find it without God or Jesus or anybody else. It's just a spot in your body. Mine happens to be right here. When you find yours, let me know and I'll be glad for you."

III

Ferguson searched for his spot but found only heartburn and hunger pains. Still, in the first month of their love he did not knowingly cheat on Annette. Once, at lunch, he took a bite of a friend's hamburger, a small bite that was already swallowed before he even realized it was meat. "After all," he explained to his friend, "you don't live twenty-eight years taking meat for granted and then automatically think 'This is meat' every time you take a bite of a hamburger, do you?"

That night Annette shunned him, but powered perhaps by that single bite of ground beef, he forced her somewhat and with sad and open eyes she suffered the carnivore upon her.

When he could not sleep, he admitted the hamburger.

"You don't have to explain, Ferguson. I knew it. I can see meat in someone I love like an x-ray. It poisons the air."

"One lousy bite can't be that poisonous," he protested.

Annette closed her eyes, pulled the nylon comforter over her like a shawl, and slept soundly beside the guilty Ferguson.

IV

By the third month he was one hundred fifty-five and shrinking. He poked ragged new holes in his belt with a kitchen knife and the extra piece of leather at the front flapped against his empty stomach. Even his shoes were too wide. His friends at first told him to see a doctor, then they said a psychiatrist. Annette expressed no pride in him but she did not reject him either. They continued that bliss they had begun at the supermarket. Away from her he sometimes felt an overpowering hunger which he soothed with cold water and occasional peanuts. In her presence the hunger was no problem. Annette Grim had taken him one step further into the nature of life. The old Ferguson would not have quibbled with "You are what you eat." The new Ferguson would roll his eyes heavenward and in a low sweet voice, not really meaning to correct you, would say, "You are what you don't eat." *Feast Not, Want Not* she calligraphed in her own hand as a decoration for the wall of his office.

"Counting the time needed for consuming and properly digesting red meat, a person spends twenty percent of his day on this single occupation. Another ten percent, say, on the body-cleaning functions needed by meat eaters in civilized society, and at least another ten percent sleeping time caused by too much amino acid combined with loss of oxygen, and you have a carnivore actually losing forty percent of his day to meat. Thus, so called convenience foods are an absolute necessity. They are to the modern meat eater what fire was to his apelike ancestors. You and I, Ferguson," she went on, "have forty percent more time; that's like adding twenty years to your life expectancy. What better thing to do for someone you love?"

Ferguson, who was a CPA and attended law classes at night, decided pragmatically that the only better thing was to marry her and spend the extra twenty years of life expectancy together in a vegetarian home of their own. When he proposed they were in her apartment on a soft couch with a broken spring which forced Ferguson to sit straighter than he wanted to and added to his nervousness. They were snacking on sunflower seeds after coming home from the movies.

When he asked, Annette closed her eyes and touched her spot. Ferguson, while he awaited her answer, imagined their first child, a girl thin as a moonbeam, lustrous of skin, jumping rope, almost popping the bands of gravity as she floated above the cracking white pavement crowded with grimy infants.

Annette, with fingertips pressed beneath her right breast, took the measure of an organ that sat within her, absolutely parallel to the heart and functioning to interpret the steady rhythms of her heart across the vastness of the chest and the many pitfalls of the digestive tract. She was solemn and her eyelids fluttered against the pressures of choice. When she opened her eyes, her voice was steady. Her spot spoke to her and it said, No—not yet, at least. "I have this strange feeling that even though I love you too, we aren't ready for each other: not yet, maybe someday. We can't push it." He knew her well enough to keep from protesting. "I don't think it can ever work out permanently until you have your spot too. It's an uncanny thing. I can't tell you what it is, but I know it's there and it only partly"—she looked sadder now than he had ever seen her—"it only partly has to do with what you eat or don't eat."

V

Something changed after the proposal. They were no longer the people who had met in the supermarket, who shared one another and a philosophy of diet. They were potential parents, potential owners of houses, cars, and major appliances. She lived in a furnished apartment, owned only a few garments, and refused to be proud of him for graduating, finally, from the South Texas College of Law after five and one half years of night-school study. He went alone to the graduation banquet, to celebrate with his classmates, their spouses, and the dean of the college. Annette stayed in her apartment working on the rug which she had been making during the months of their romance.

"Enjoy yourself," she said as he left, wrinkling her tiny nose, smiling as if to tease him for going to a steakhouse to celebrate what she called "thousands of hours of studying dullness." According to Annette it was a fitting celebration. Ferguson and fifty-five fat, hard-working Texas night-school lawyers going out to munch upon the loins of cattle in a restaurant decorated like a covered wagon.

"I'll bring you back the bone," he said, feeling cruel and smug

himself. This was their first real fight. She might not find anything worth praising in his past, but this one night with people
who had shared his ambition in countless humid hours while
night settled over Houston and the red neon sign of the beauty
academy across the street peeped through the venetian blinds,
this one night with his fellow law students she would not rob
him of. It had nothing to do with food. He planned to eat fruitplate. It had been ordered for him by the banquet chairman
weeks before.

Ferguson sat three chairs from the dean, shared in toasts to the
college, to the dean, to the wives and families of these working
men whose sacrifices had made daddy, against long odds, a lawyer.
Ferguson felt especially cheated not having someone to clink his
champagne glass with. Even the dean brought a wife. After they
had toasted the Law itself, a cowgirl waitress placed in front of
Ferguson 'Sonny's Special,' a ten-inch medium-rare filet, butter-
flied so that it spread open like a radish, exposing its sizzling
innards. "I ordered fruitplate," he told her, but she was well
along the table and his voice fell among the sound of plates and
teeth meeting beef. Goddamn, Ferguson said to himself, and he
sliced off a bite of the steak, hesitated, chewed, and when he saw
that it was good, he ate with relish and a pinch of A-1 sauce the
remainder of Sonny's Special, had an after-dinner liqueur and
two cups of coffee. He thought he must look like a snake who
had swallowed a whole piglet, but in the men's room mirror,
his stomach did not bulge. On the contrary, his skin had a ruddy
healthy glow he had not seen in some time. "If she can't celebrate
one lousy night with me after my five and a half years, then the
hell with her," he told his reflection.

He went home, not to her apartment and her x-ray senses. Not
that Ferguson intended to hide the steak from her. He would
admit it but without feeling guilty. He paid enough that night
for his gluttony on a stomach accustomed for three months to
vegetables.

In the morning she was gone, disappeared, evanesced as if she
had never been there. The door was open, a yogurt carton
scraped clean lay alone in the garbage bag. The cupboard empty,

the refrigerator empty, open, unplugged, smelling baking-powder clean. The bare hangers in her closet looked to Ferguson like bright teeth in a corpse. He ran to the building supervisor, who told him, "Mizz Grim left real early in the morning in a taxicab. She gave her two weeks notice and cleaned the place up good."

At the Prudential Insurance building Ferguson learned the same. Annette Grim, who for more than a year typed policy amendments five days a week, had given a two-week advance notice and told the girl at the desk next to her that she was going to Dallas. For several hours Ferguson sat in the Prudential coffee shop trying to make himself get up from his small table and his cold cup of tea, but he could not leave until he knew where to go. "What about our camping trip?" he asked aloud. He put his head on the table and breathed deeply, hoping the oxygen would clear his head. His body was sluggish from the meat and wine of the banquet. He finally decided to go home and hope she would be there to tell him this was her joking way of saying, yes, she wanted to get married right this minute. She had quit her job so that they could start a family immediately, even before the camping trip.

But Ferguson's apartment was as empty as it had always been, and he, three months a lover and a vegetarian, four days a lawyer, and all his life a loner, sat down with a bowl of wheat germ and milk to contemplate the suddenly narrow vista of his future. Annette was, after all, not his. Only a handful of people even knew about them as a couple.

Thanks to his law degree, Shell Oil would move him on Monday from accounting to contracts. Without Annette the weekend looming before him seemed longer than the twenty added years of life expectancy which she had bequeathed to him as a free gift. He spent Saturday and Sunday in a total fast, re-examining his months with Annette, and found no clues to her sudden departure. The two weeks' notice to her landlord and to the Prudential suggested that Annette had well-laid plans, but this, Ferguson understood, was a guise. She did not fool him. He knew, in spite of the apparent facts, that had he not left her for that Thursday night banquet he would not be alone now. Had he gone to the banquet and at least not eaten the steak, that too might have been enough to sustain their love.

But he had gone and he had eaten, and the beef that passed through him came between them, perhaps forever. Ferguson arose from his two-day fast and prepared to seek within himself the spot that would solve the mystery of Annette and create the Ferguson she could live with.

VI

The lawyer waned. After the initial fast, he worked out his own penance. For thirty days he would do the brown-rice regimen. A diet that Annette said was okay but too austere and too low on fluids. For thirty days he would eat only the king of grains, brown rice with its perfect harmony of phosphorous and potassium. He prepared it in a pressure cooker so that it took only a few minutes to cook and lasted days. Finding no comfort in friends and in no mood for entertainment, Ferguson worked late on the Shell leases and lost weight. His plan was to use these thirty days of brown rice in two ways. First to cleanse his body from that meat orgy of the banquet, and second to hope that in some mysterious way his monkish diet would be communicated to Annette, who would forgive and return. When at the end of thirty days she had not returned, he put away the pressure cooker and resumed a more normal vegetarian diet. He was now down to one hundred forty-seven and had to buy some smaller-sized clothes.

His new boss, the head of Shell contracts, called him "the most dedicated young man I've ever seen," and took Ferguson to lunch in the executive dining room, where amid martini-drinking businessmen and special cuts of aged beef the dedicated young man ate, at company expense, a lettuce and avocado salad. "You're too thin," said the head of contracts; "have a roast-beef sandwich. It's Iowa beef." Ferguson smiled his thanks and rejected chicken salad as well.

He was beginning to realize that he might just have to get

over her, that whatever diet or other penance he tried might
not do it. After all, thirty-four days and not even a post card
to a man who had virtually lived with you for three months, who
had proposed and told you all his heart. Thirty-four days of
silence when she knew how barren he was without her. This he
did not deserve for one steak. She knew it, he knew it. It was
something else.

VII

At one hundred forty-two pounds, Ferguson began to have
mild hallucinations. Nothing colorful or spectacular, no dream-
like surreal dazzlers, only short episodic vignettes slightly more
concrete than a daydream. It was as if, all at once, the characters
in the daydream had a bright spotlight focused upon them. The
light did not deter them. They went about their business, but it
made Ferguson recognize the subtle difference between a daydream and a hallucination. There was nothing terrifying in these
experiences, and he felt, in spite of his thinness, healthy and
robust. The hallucinations were largely about oil and taxes. In
the first episode that he recognized as a new phenomenon, the
daydream was Ferguson as a Shell executive somewhere upon a
Colorado slope looking over thousands of green acres beneath
which there might be recoverable shale deposits. The scene was
as standard as a poster. When it became a hallucination, the
earth slowly opened, disturbing nothing on the surface, and
droplets of oil shot up like slippery watermelon seeds. As far as
the oilman could see, this happened, the droplets flying up
rhythmically like coffee percolating. No results, only the image,
and Ferguson was back reading the fine print in a Shell lease
between Mr. Howard S. Sounders of Ardmore, Oklahoma, and
the Company, regarding section 71 and adjoining properties
of McClehlen's addition, Runyn County.

The episodes followed no pattern and happened at home as
well as at the office. He considered seeing a doctor but he
suspected the doctor would suggest psychotherapy, and Fer-

guson, though he might be in despair and loneliness, felt very certain of his sanity. Anyway, how explain to a doctor that you were hoping to find within yourself a hidden resource called a spot which had a true and absolute physical existence and yet might vary in location among peoples and had never been located in an autopsy. "Doctors look for causes of disease," Annette had once told him when they discussed her spot, "doctors look for causes of death; this is a cause of life." Although Ferguson disliked the mumbo jumbo of mysticism, he did not think the idea of a spot was so absurd. The analogy with nature was very clear to him. All sorts of land looked the same from the surface, only a good geologist could tell you exactly where to drill for oil. Life itself starting with one cell spread to many. Scientists were continually finding out the secret codes of genetic reproduction. A person's spot would one day also be labeled, perhaps called an I AM, a fingernail of an RNA itself a fingernail of a DNA, and all this history pummeling through you with so little commotion that, if you don't stop to look for it, it might lie undisturbed, like oil, for millions of years. Perhaps most people didn't need a spot, they were still in a spotless age, the way men for thousands of generations didn't need oil or uranium even though it was always there just waiting to be needed. Because of Annette Grim Ferguson needed his spot. She was the catalyst that had moved Ferguson, of necessity, beyond the frontiers of science. Doctors could not help, nor because of the personal and secular nature of the spot could theologians or friends or entertainment or art. Thus, Ferguson ate fruits, vegetables, grains, seeds, and lowfat milk products, did his work for Shell Oil, and hoped for a better life.

VIII

To help him find his spot, Ferguson tried, in order, yoga, transcendental meditation, dynamic tension, and aerobics. Nothing did it, but after some experimentation with these methods of body analysis and muscle control, he found certain combinations that offered, if not a spot, at least some release from his anxieties. He could combine the jogging with the dynamic tension by squeezing his hands together as he ran. The tension squirted from his palms down to his legs and was dissipated in a seven-minute mile. It surprised Ferguson that, even though he was losing all hope of ever regaining Annette, he had no desire to go back to his old eating habits. Meat had forever joined the ranks of certain other inedible materials, wood, steel, fabric, glass. For her he sought his spot, for himself he remained a vegetarian.

IX

When he reached one hundred thirty-four, Ferguson's entire aspect changed. He had apparently exhausted all the extra flesh that had remained in his cheeks, and suddenly his face looked as strong and bony as a fist. His forehead, his cheekbones, his nose, and his chin stood out like the knuckles in a clenched hand. Sixty pounds ago Ferguson had been round cheeked, almost teddy bearish in appearance. A few girls had liked him because he was cute and cuddly. Now he had become an arrowhead.

Because he could concentrate with such perfect composure and for so long a time, Ferguson did the work of five men. In hours he read through the contracts that took other lawyers days or weeks, and he rarely made even the smallest of errors. In the office they called him the computer, but as he continued to shrink they changed his name to Pocket Calculator. His eyes soared out of the bleak landscape of his face. They sought Annette the way birds seek out a resting place after long journeys. Because Ferguson's bird eyes found no Annette they did not rest. He could awaken from ten hours of perfect slumber with sleepless, raging eyes. And these remembering eyes became the great weight of his body. When they blinked long, he might lose his balance and sway in the wind. He thought of himself as a simplified diagram. There was a plumb line extending directly from his eyes down to his mouth, his belly, and his penis, and upward to his brain. The line was taut and powerful. Yet something was missing, a spot as intricate and important as any other in the brain-to-penis complex.

At night after deep breathing exercises in the lotus position and a three-minute shoulder stand, Ferguson would lie completely still in his bed and examine the front of his body as if the examining fingers belonged to someone else. He would speak aloud to himself as the finger doctors did their checking of the clean and relaxed corpus under them. "Here," the digits would pound at the solar plexus, "perhaps it is here, where it hurts when I poke, here, in this little Mesopotamia between the lungs." The fingers would pound at the space between his ribs until he could barely catch his breath, but no inkling of the spot. As far as the finger doctors could reach, they touched and examined and tried to root out the spot. And when all else failed, the doctors became Annette. They found out his most obvious weakness and pulled away at his solid flesh until it melted and stained Ferguson with the realization of his loneliness.

X

Mr. Solomon, his boss in the contracts department, insisted that Ferguson take a two-week vacation. "Longer if you like," he said, "and of course with full pay. You've done a year's work in a few months, go out and relax, have some fun." Solomon slapped him on the back in a broad gesture of camaraderie. But as he shook Ferguson's hand and pulled him closer the older lawyer said in a voice of honest concern, "Son, is there anything I can do to help you? Whatever it is, I know you won't talk about it, but I just want you to know that Harold Solomon cares. You're the best contracts man here, but I don't give a damn about that when I can see you suffering right in front of me. Do something about it on this vacation, son, and when you come back remember that Harold Solomon isn't just your boss, he's your friend."

Mr. Solomon's concern touched Ferguson but it also unnerved him. He realized for the first time how obvious his despair must be. It was five and one half months since the banquet. He weighed one hundred twenty-eight pounds now and domestic dress shirts ballooned around his chest. He switched to the modish handmade type, mostly Indian, which hung loosely over his shoulders and gave him the look of a very large and well-groomed Asian peasant. On the first day of his vacation, he took the Greyhound bus to Dallas, checked into the Holiday Inn under the name of William Glass, and rented a car. He could have driven his own car and registered under his own name. He did not understand why he acted so irrationally, but he decided to follow his whims and hope that they would lead him to Annette.

Ferguson did not roam the streets of Dallas looking for her, but he sought out the health-food shops and the vegetarian restaurants where he thought she might be. He had no photograph to pass around and her description—thin, fair, strong, beautiful, direct, knowledgeable, precise, self-assured—none of this really described her. Annette Grim was identifiable only by her spot, that roommate of her heart, which sat beneath her solemn nipple on the right-hand side of an otherwise biologically unspectacular chest. "I am probably in better condition than she is," Ferguson thought; "she probably doesn't run and do yoga." Perhaps he could even teach her something new.

In a restaurant called Pelops Arms, beneath a modern cartoon of Greek heroes wrestling with monsters, Ferguson sat eating an avocado, cheese, and mung-sprout sandwich. Dallas had even fewer health restaurants than Houston. In the midst of men who raised cattle for shipment to the dinner tables of America, there sat Ferguson eschewing red meats, disdaining poultry, laying off eggs, hardening and slenderizing a body that sought its own center, and while doing so rushed with all its pent-up energies toward unknown places, creating, like the universe itself, an area of empty space wherever it traveled. There sat Ferguson, just and thin and powerful, seeking his center like a dog after its own tail.

"Pardon me," the voice said, and Ferguson's raging eyes turned as always, looking for her, frightening by their intensity an innocent waitress delivering a bill for $1.79.

"Was everything all right?" she asked.

"Are you in a hurry?" Ferguson asked her in return.

She smiled at the empty restaurant. "You're the only customer," she said, and sat down opposite him. Starting from the
day in the supermarket, Ferguson told her almost everything.
This girl, Kathleen Simpson, a junior at SMU, herself not completely vegetarian, sat in awe as the story of Ferguson's search for
a spot unfolded before her.

"I never heard of anything like it," she said, "but I believe in
the soul so it is not so preposterous to me. I'm through here in an
hour, I'll help you look. There's only a few places in Dallas
where a girl like that might be and they're not far from here."
Ferguson paid his $1.79 and sipped distilled water while he
waited for Kathleen. She took him to the Garden of Eden, where
long-haired men sold grain and seeds out of huge tin pails. She
led him to the Cornucopia, which catered to SMU students and
served only a modest vegetarian choice amid a wide meat menu.
Caesar's Salad, a small downtown coffee shop that served luncheon
greens to secretaries, was the only other place she could think of.
Annette, of course, was in none of these restaurants, but since she
had been a secretary, Ferguson thought this last one might be a
good place for him to camp out and wait for her. Kathleen Simpson, brown eyed and friendly, wished him well.

The next day Ferguson haunted Caesar's Salad. It was very
difficult to stay there for long. There was only a counter with
eight stools and three small booths that at lunch and with squeezing could accommodate four each. Twenty customers maximum
and two waitresses. By noon both of them knew Ferguson and
suspected him. He explained but they asked him to do his waiting outside. Ferguson stood in the Dallas sun trying to shade
himself beneath the awning of a nearby paint store. From the
store window a cardboard peacock flashed many colors into the
sunlight, dazzling him. He took a salt tablet and carried a paper
cup of water with him, but the Dallas afternoon rose above
one hundred and Ferguson felt weak and dizzy. He visited, on
foot, the only Dallas landmark he knew, the place of the school-
book depository and the grassy knoll. As he walked the route
of the motorcade he tried to imagine the sound of the bullets,

the scream of Jacqueline, Lyndon Johnson, fearful beneath a secret-service man. The book depository had been torn down, the grassy knoll was merely an overpass for a highway, and a small plaque marked the place where the President's head had been splintered.

For the first time Ferguson wondered about the spots of the great. Did someone like President Kennedy have a spot which he consulted when the Russians put missiles in Cuba? Had there been an inkling, a negative feeling, like Annette had about him, on that day in November when the young President put on his clean starched shirt, his cuff links and his garters, and shook his longish hair in front of the mirror to make certain that it would look fine in the hot Dallas wind? If important people had spots and listened to them, things would not go wrong in the world, Ferguson reasoned. Yet starting from himself and stretching right to the farthest astronaut hitting a golf ball on the moon, there was a line of chaos as direct as the plumb line that went through Ferguson. Who had absolutes? Even the Pope changed his mind. Only his Annette heard the hum of the rhythm of her body, while a tone-deaf world scrambled around her.

"I have tried," Ferguson said aloud in the shadow of the grassy knoll where thousands had watched the motorcade speed up and curve toward Parkland Hospital; "I have fasted and meditated and relentlessly examined myself. I have known no strangers among women, nor have my lips touched the flesh of birds or animals." The desert heat struck him full force as he raised his face heavenward and saw for an instant the flaming sun, like a carbonated peacock bubbling in his eyes. He shielded himself with uplifted arms, and a Buick whisked by so closely that the string tie of his shirt thudded softly against the outside mirror of the automobile.

"Watch yourself, nut," the driver yelled back at him.

"I have been doing that," Ferguson answered, "I have been doing little else." To the grassy knoll and to the anonymous traffic Ferguson announced, "I know myself and have no spot. Kennedy had none, neither did Roosevelt, or Justice Frankfurter, or George Washington." Ferguson raced up the grassy knoll and proclaimed to the roaring highway, "You lost me too, Annette. Whoever you're huddled with now does not love you like I did. You were my spot and your spot didn't know it."

In the Dallas heat he ran along the side of the highway in his long-and-easy jogging stride. Along Dallas Avenue Ferguson ran, past post-office buildings and skyscrapers, through streets emptied by the hot sun. As he ran he clenched and unclenched his fists, letting the dynamic tension pulse through his arms as the crashing cement vibrated through his legs. Deeply he inhaled the city, its desert air and its poisonous oxides. As his ribcage stretched, Ferguson felt loose and lucid. He imagined that the plumb line was now stretched taut, that the final open space had been pulled out with a sudden jerk and had disappeared, leaving him unmarked down the middle. He raced past Caesar's Salad not even casting a glance. His second wind had come by the time Ferguson reached Pelops Arms. Entering at a gallop, he surprised Kathleen Simpson, who handed him distilled water.

"Did you find her?" she asked.

"Yes," Ferguson said, "will you run with me?"

"Where?"

"To Houston for dinner, and then through Mexico to the Pan American Highway, along the banks of the Amazon, over the Chilean Andes right into Buenos Aires."

Kathleen hesitated, then she slipped off her short black apron, put down her green order pad, and in a long and fluent stride, side by side with Ferguson, headed south.

Inside
Norman
Mailer

I

So what if I could kick the shit out of Truman Capote, and who really cares that once in a Newark bar, unknown to each other, I sprained the wrist of E. L. Doctorow in a harmless arm wrestle. For years I've kicked around in out-of-the-way places, sparred for a few bucks or just for kicks with the likes of Scrap Iron Johnson, Phil Rahv, Kenny Burke, and Chico Vejar. But, you know, I'm getting older too. When I feel the quick arthritic pains fly through my knuckles, I ask myself, Where are your poems and novels? Where are your long-limbed girls with cunts like tangerines? Yes, I've had a few successes. There are towns in America where people recognize me on the street and ask what I'm up to these days. "I'm thirty-three," I tell them, "in the top of my form. I'm up to the best. I'm up to Norman Mailer."

They think I'm kidding, but the history of our game is speckled with the unlikely. Look at Pete Rademacher—not even a pro. Fresh from a three-round Olympic decision, he got a shot at Floyd Patterson, made the cover of *Sports Illustrated*, picked up an easy hundred grand. Now that is one fight that Mr. Mailer, the literary lion, chose not to discuss. The clash between pro and amateur didn't grab his imagination like two spades in Africa or the dark passion of Emile Griffith. Yes, you know how to pick your spots, Norman. I who have studied your moves think that your best instinct is judgment. It's your secret punch. You knew how to stake out Kennedy and Goldwater, but on the whole you kept arm's length from Nixon. Humphrey never earned you a dime.

Ali, the moon, scrappy broads, dirty walls, all meat to you, slugger. But even Norman Mailer has misplayed a few. Remember the Chassidic tales? The rabbi pose was one you couldn't quite pull off, but you cut your losses fast, the mark of a real pro, and I fully expect that you'll come back to that one yet to cash in big on theology. Maybe at sixty you'll throw a birthday party for yourself in the Jerusalem Hilton. You'll roll up in an ancient scroll, grow earlocks, and say, "This is the big one, the one I've been waiting for." With Allen Ginsberg along on a leash you'll clank through the holy cities living on nuts and distilled water and sell your films as a legitimate appendix to the New Testament.

If I had the patience I'd wait for that religious revival and be your Boswell, then I'd drive off that whole crew of trainers and seconds who tag after you, but by then I'll be almost fifty and maybe too slow to do you justice. As the rabbis said: "Reputation is a meal, energy a food stamp." It's *toches affen tisch*, you understand that, big boy? I'm spotting you seventy pounds, a dozen books, wives, children, memories, millions in the bank. My weapons are desperation, neglect, and bad form. I am the C student in a mediocre college, the madman in the crowd, the quaint gunman who rides into Dodge City because he's heard they have good restaurants. We share only a mutual desire to let it all take place in public, in the open. This is the way Mailer has always played it, this I learned from you. Why envy from afar when I can pummel you in a lighted ring. Your reputation makes it possible. You who are composed of genes and risks, you appreciate the wildness of strangers. Anyway, you think you'll nail me in one.

While I, for months, have been running fifteen miles a day and eating natural food, you train by scratching your nuts with a soft rubber eraser. You take walks in the moonlight and turn the clichés inside out. For you they make way. Sidewalks tilt, lovers quarrel. People whisper your name to each other, give you wholesale prices and numerous gifts. An "Okay" from Norman

Mailer makes a career. Power like this there has not been since Catullus in old Rome carried on his instep Caesar's daughter.

I'll give you this much: you have come by it honestly. Not by bribery and not by marriage, not by family ties and not by wealth, not by good luck alone or by the breaks of the game. You have plenty, Slugger, that I'll admit. But I do not come at you like a barbarian. The latest technology is in my corner. The Schick 1000-watt blow-dryer, trunks by Haspel, robe by Mr. Mann, Jovan cologne. Adidas kidskin shoes travel three quarters of my shin with laces of mandarin silk. From my flesh, coated with Vaseline and Desenex, the sweat breaks forth like pearls. My desperation grows muscular in the bright lights. I am the fatted calf.

You stand in your corner like Walt Whitman. No electric outlets, cheap cotton YMCA trunks, even your gloves look used. Your red robe just says "Norm." You wear sneakers and no socks. I should take you the Oriental way by working your feet up to blisters and then stepping on your toes, but I lack the Chinaman's patience. No, it will have to be head to head, although everyone has cautioned me about trading punches with you.

Last week a crowd of critics came out to my camp in a chartered bus. They carried canes and magnifying glasses. They told me to evaluate each punch from the shoulder. "Let your elbow be the judge," Robert Penn Warren said; "Sting like an irony," from Booth of Chicago. They told me that if I win I'll get an honorary degree from Kenyon and a job at one of the best gyms in the Midwest. Like a Greek chorus they stood beside my training ring and sang in unison, "Don't slug it out, move and think. Speed and reflexes beat out power. To the victor goes the victory."

"Scram," I yelled, spitting my between-the-rounds mouthwash. "Get lost you crummy bastards. You shit on my poems and laughed off my stories, now you want some of my body language. Go study the ambiguities of Harold Robbins." I was mad as hell but they stood firm taking notes on my weight and reach. Finally a group of kids carrying "Free Rubin Carter" signs ran them back to the bus.

The press is no help either. They are so tired of promoting

Ali against a bunch of nobodies that to them I'm just another Joe Bugner. They rarely call me by name. "Mailer's latest victim to be" is their tag. The *Times* calls me a "man with little to recommend him. Slight, almost feline, with the gestures of a minor poet, this latest in a long series of Mailer baiters seems to have no more business in the ring with the master than Stan Ketchel had with Jack Johnson. No one is interested in this fight. The Astrodome will be bare, UHF refuses to televise, and Mailer has scheduled a reading for later that night at the University of Houston. Norman, why do you keep accepting every challenge from the peanut gallery? Let's stop this Christians versus Lions until there is a real contender. Now, if the Pynchon backers could come up with a site and a solid guarantee, that might be a real match."

You know what I say, I say, "Fuck the *Times*." They gave Clay no chance against Big Bad Sonny Liston, and four years later the "meanest, toughest" champ the *Times* ever saw dropped dead while tying his shoes and Muhammad built a Temple for Elijah M. So much for the sports writers.

But there are a few people who understand. Teddy White will be in my corner and Senator Proxmire at ringside. *The Realist* and the L.A. *Free Press* have picked me. The DAR sent a fruit basket. Outside the literary crowd I'm actually well liked. Cesar Chavez and the migrants from South Texas are coming up to cheer for me and my friend Ira from Minneapolis and the whole English department of my school. All the Democratic Presidential candidates sent telegrams; so did Bill Buckley, Mayor Beame, Gore Vidal, Irving Wallace, John Ehrlichman, and Herman Kahn.... All I can say is, when the time comes boys, I'll be ready, just watch.

II

Our first face-to-face meeting is at the weigh-in. He wanted to dispense with it and turn in a morning urine specimen instead. The boxing commission put the nix on that idea. Oh, he knew

who I was before the weigh-in. We had traded photos, autographs, and once I had anthologized him. But face to face on
either side of a big metal scale with our robes on and Teddy
White rubbing my back while I stare bullets, that is something
else again.

He nods, I look away. He can afford to be gracious. If I win,
I'll make a handsome donation to UNICEF in his honor. For
now, I button my lip. He chats with White about convention
sites, claims that because of tonight he'll have an insider's edge
if they do the '76 one in the Astrodome.

I come in at one hundred forty-four and three quarters, thirty-
four-inch reach. He is two hundred fourteen and a thirty-inch
reach. He spots me the reach and eighteen years. I give him seventy pounds and a ton of reputation. He has enough grace under
pressure to teach at a ballet school, but the smile discloses bad
teeth. I'll remember that. His body hairs are graying. I can see
that he has not trained and could use sleep. My tongue lies at
the bottom of my mouth. "Good luck, kid," he says, but I have
removed my contact lenses and only learn later that it was the
Great One in a magnanimous gesture whom I snubbed because
I had to take a leak.

III

The Dome is a half-empty cave. At the last minute they lowered
all tickets to a buck, and thousands popped in to see the King.
To me the crowd means nothing. It is as anonymous as the whir
of an air conditioner. I stare at the Everlast trademark on my
gloves and practice keeping the mouthpiece in without gagging.
"Stay loose," Teddy yells over the din, "stay loose as a goose and
box like a fox."

I dance in my corner for three or four minutes before he
appears. The crowd goes wild when that woolly head jogs up the
ramp. He climbs through the ropes and goes to center ring. He
throws kisses with both open gloves. He is wearing the same
YMCA trunks and cheap sneakers, but his robe is a threadbare

terrycloth without a name. It looks like something he picked up at Goodwill on the way over. The crowd loves his slovenliness.

"To each his own," I whisper to myself as I ask Teddy for a final hit with the blow-dryer. My curls are tight as iron; his hang like eggshells crowding around his ears. He throws a kiss to me; I try to return it with the finger but my glove makes it a hand.

The referee motions us to center ring. We both requested Ruby Goldstein but the old pro wouldn't come out of retirement for a match like this one. I then asked for the Brown Bomber and Mailer wanted Jersey Joe. Finally we compromised on Archie Moore, who has a goatee now and is wearing a yellow leisure suit as he calls us together for a review of the rules. I notice that he is wearing street shoes and think to protest, but I see that he needs the black patent pumps in order to make his trousers break at the step. A good sign, I think. Archie will be with me.

He goes over the mandatory eight count and the three-knock-down rule, but Mailer and I ignore the words. Our eyes meet and mine are ready for his. For countless hours I have trained before a mirror with his snapshot taped to the middle. I have had blown up to poster size that old *Esquire* pose of him in the ring, and I am ready for what I know will be the first real encounter. My eyes are steady on his. In the first few seconds I see boredom, I see sweet brown eyes that would open into yawning mouthlike cavities if they could. I see indifferent eyes and gay youthful glances. Checkbook eyes. Evelyn Wood eyes. Then suddenly he blinks and I have my first triumph. Fear pops out. Plain old unabashed fear. Not trembling, not panic, just a little fear. And I've found it in the eyes, exactly like the nineteenth-century writers used to before Mailer switched it to the asshole. I smile and he knows that I know. Anger replaces the fear but the edge is mine, big boy. All the sportswriters and oddsmakers haven't lulled you. You know that every time you step into the ring it's like going to the doctor with a slight cough that with a little twist of the DNA turns out to be cancer. You, old cancer-monger, you know this better than anyone. In my small frame, in my gleaming slightly feline gestures you have smelled the blood test, the chest x-ray, the specialist, the lies, the operations, the false hopes, the statistics. Yes, Norman, you looked at me or through me and in some distant future that maybe I carry in my hands like a telegram, there you glimpsed that old bugaboo and it went straight to your prostate, to your bladder, and to your heavy fingertips. In a second, Norm, you built me up. Oh, I have grown big on your fear. Giant killers have to so that they can reach up for the fatal stab to the heart.

No camera has recorded this. Nor has Archie Moore repeating his memorized monologue noted our exchange. Only you and I, Norm, understand. This is as it should be. You have given dignity to my challenge; like a sovereign government you have recognized my hopeless revolutionary state and turned me, in a blink, credible, at least to you, at least where it counts. I slap my fists together and at the bell I meet you for the first time as an equal.

IV

The problem now is as old as realism. You don't want all the grunts, the shortness of breath, the sound of leather on skin, and I don't want to tell you in great detail. But its all there, the throwing of punches, the clinches, the head butting, the swelling of injured faces. If I forget to, then you put it in. For I am too busy taking the measure of my opponent to feel the slap of his glove against my flesh. The bell has moved us into a new field of force. We drop our pens. The spotlight is the glare of eternity, and what it has all come to is simply the matter of Truth. "Existentialist" I call him, spitting out my mouthpiece, though in practice I have recited Peter Piper a dozen times and kept the mouthpiece in. "Dated existentialist. Insincere existentialist. Jewish existentialist . . ." I hit him with this smooth combination, but he continues to rush me bearlike, serene, full of skill and power.

"Campy lightweight," he yells, in full charge as I sidestep his rush and he tangles his upper body in the ropes.

I come up behind, and as well as I can with the gross movement of the glove I pull back his head and expose the blue gnarled cacophony of his neck.

"I am Abraham and you the ram caught in the thicket," I announce from behind. "I have been an outcast in many lands, I bear the covenant, and you full of power and goatish lust, you carry the false demon out of whose curved horn I will blow my own triumph and salvation."

"How unlike an Abraham thou art," he responds, gasping from his entanglement in the ropes. "Where is thy son then and where thy handmaiden Hagar, whom thou so ungenerously got with a child of false promise and then discarded into the wilderness? Thou art an assumer of historical identities, a chameleon of literary pretension."

I reach into the empty air for the sword of slaughter when Archie Moore separates us, rights Mailer, and warns me about hair pulling and exposing the jugular of my opponent.

Now we stalk one another at center ring. He, not having trained, not having rested, not having regarded my challenge as serious, he is ready almost at once to revert to instinctive behavior. He wants it all animal now and tries to bite off his glove so that he can come at me with ten fingers. But I am still in the airy realms of the mind. I see and discern his actions. How coarse appears the Mailer saliva upon his worn gloves, how disgusting his tongue and crooked teeth as they nibble at the strings. His mouth has become as a loom with the glove lace moving between his teeth on the slow, feeble power of his tongue.

"The Industrial Revolution," I yell across the ring, and his gloves drop, his mouth is open and agape. I land a hard right to his jaw and feel the ligaments stretch. At the bell he is dazed and hurt. He moves to his corner like an old man in an unemployment line.

I stand in the middle of the ring and watch the slow shuffle toward comfort of this man whom most enlightened folks thought I could not withstand for even three minutes. So carefully have I trained, so honest has been my fifteen miles of daily roadwork that the first round of exertion has scarcely left me breathless. While Norman is in his corner swishing his mouth, having his brow mopped, I am in mid-ring, stunned with my opening achievement. I have stayed a full round with him. I have seen the fear in his eyes and the beast in his soul. I have felt the heft of his sweating form in a heavy embrace. In the clinch, as our protective cups clicked against each other, there have I surmised his lust. For three metaphysical moments we two white men have embraced in violence while old black Archie pares his perfect fingernails in the midst of us.

"Don't forget the game plan," Teddy is yelling from my corner. He wants my help in pulling the blackboard through the ropes. I come out of my reverie to help him. Oh, I have been waiting for this moment, and now but for good old Teddy I might have forgotten. Like the most careful teacher printing large block letters for an eager second grade, I inscribe and turn to four sides so all can see, "The Naked and the Dead Is His Best Work."

When Norman reads my inscription, he is swishing Gatorade in his mouth while his second, Richard Poirier, applies with a Q-tip glycerine and rosewater to the Mailer lips. When my barb registers, he swallows the Gatorade and bites the Q-tip in half. Poirier and José Torres can barely keep him on his stool. They whisper frantically, each in an ear. Archie is across the ring getting a quick shine from a boy who manages, on tiptoe, to reach with his buffing cloth up to the apron of the elevated ring. Arch kneels to tip with an autograph.

When the bell tolls round two, I face a Mailer who has with herculean effort quickly calmed himself. He has sucked in his cheeks for control and looks, for the moment, like a tubercular housewife. I see immediately that he has beaten back the demi-urge. We will stay in the realms of the intellect. His gloves are completely laced and his steps are tight and full of control. He dances over to the ropes and beckons me with an open glove to taste his newness.

Who do you think I am, Norm? Didn't I travel half a world with no hope of writing a book about it to watch Ali lure George Foreman to the ropes? Not for me, Norm, is your coy ease along the top strand. I'll wait and take you in the open. You see, I learned more than you did in Africa. While you holed up in an air-conditioned hotel and resurrected those eight rounds for your half a million advance, I thumbed my way to what was once called Biafra. I went to the cemetery where Dick Tiger lies dead of causes unknown at age thirty-five in newly prosperous Nigeria. How did you miss Dick Tiger? You who were the first white negro, you the crown prince of nigger-lovers, you missed the ace of the jungle. Yes, he was the heart of the dark continent, the Aristotle of Africa. A middleweight and a revolutionary. While you clowned around with Torres and Ali and Emile Griffith, Tiger packed his gear and headed home to see what he could pick clean from the starvation and the slaughter. He went home to face bad times and bad people and was dead a week after his plane touched down. Where were you and the sportswriters, Norm, when Dick Tiger needed you? I at least made the trek to the resting place of the hero, and it was there in the holy calm of his forgotten tomb that I vowed to come back and make my move. No one offered me a penny for "The Dick Tiger Story" as told to me, so you won't get it now either. Come out to the middle, Norm. No, you're still coy, relaxed; well, two can play that one.

I sit down in the corner opposite him; I fan myself with the mouthpiece. To the audience it looks as if we're kidding. He sloping against the ropes, I twenty-five feet away pretending I'm at a picnic in the English countryside. Real fight fans know what's up. There is only a certain amount of available energy. In the universe it's called entropy; in the ring it is known as "ppf," punches per flurry. Neither of us has the strength at this moment to muster the necessary ten to twelve ppf's to really damage the other. Fighters trained in the Golden Gloves or various homes for juvenile delinquents will go through the motions anyway. They will stalk and butt and sweat upon each other. But Mailer and I, knowing the score, wait out the round. Archie Moore leafs through the Texas Boxing Commission rules. Some fans boo, others take advantage of the lull to refresh themselves.

For me, every second is a victory. Round by round I wear the laurel and the bay. Who thought I could even last the first? Five will get me tenure, seven and I'll be a dean. Yes, I can wait, Norm, until you come to me in mid-ring with all that bulk and experience. Come to me with your strength, your wisdom, your compassion, and your insight. This time at the bell we are both giggling, aware each to each of the resined canvas upon which we paint our destinies.

I walk over to his corner where he sits on his stool, kingly again, not hurt as he was after round one. He offers me a drink from his green bottle. We spit into the same bucket. I know his seconds don't like me coming over there between rounds. Poirier turns away but Norman smiles, cuffs me playfully behind the neck. Together we walk out to await the bell.

For twice three minutes we have traveled the same turf. Ambition and gravity have held us in a dialectical encounter, but as round three begins, Mailer's old friend the irrational joins us. No matter that I actually see the pig-tailed form of my sister beckoning me between mouthfuls of popcorn to rush at you. Aeneas, Hector, Dick Tiger, they too saw the phantoms that promise the sunshine and delight after one quick lunge. My sister is nine years old. She wears a gingham dress. She is right there beside you, close enough for Archie to stumble on.

"Watch out, kid," I say, "you shouldn't even be here."

"It's okay," Mailer says. "She has my permission."

She throws the empty popcorn box over the ropes. "Please take me home," she whimpers, and as she stands there the power enters me, the ppf quotient floods my own soul, and I rush, not in fear, not in anger, but in full sweet confidence, I rush with both fists to the middle of Norman Mailer.

First my left with all its quixotic force and then my sure and solid right lands in the valley of his solar plexus. Next my head in a raw, cruel butt joins the piston arms. Hands, arms, head, neck, back, legs. As a boy for the first time shakes the high dive in the presence of his parents, with such pride do I dive. And with the power of falling human weight knifing through the chlorine-dark pool do I catapult. As a surgeon lays open flesh, indifferently, thinking not of tumors but of the arc of his raquet in full backswing, with such professional ease am I engulfed.

I hear the wind leave his lungs. Like large soft earlobes, they shade me from the glare of his heart. The sound of his digestive juices is rhythmic and I resonate to the music of his inner organs. I hear the liver weakened from drink but on key still, the gentle reek of kidneys, the questioning solo of pancreas, the harmonica-like appendix, all here all around me, and the cautionary voice of my mother: "Be careful, little one, when you hit someone so hard in the stomach. That's how Houdini died."

Somewhere else Archie Moore is counting ten over a prone loser. Judges are packing up scorecards and handbags snap shut. I am comfortable in the damp prison of his rib cage. His blood explodes like little Hiroshimas every second.

"Concentrate," says Mailer, "so the experience will not be wasted on you."

"It's hard," I say, "amid the color and distraction."

"I know," says my gentle master, "but think about one big thing."

I concentrate on the new edition of the *Encyclopædia Britannica*. It works. My mind is less a palimpsest, more a blank page.

"You may be too young to remember," he says, "James Jones and James T. Farrell and James Gould Cozzens and dozens like them. I took them all on, absorbed all they had and went on my way, just like Shakespeare ate up *Tottel's Miscellany*." (

"No lectures," I gasp, "only truths."

"I am the Twentieth Century," Mailer says. "Go forth from here toward the east and earn your bread by the sweat of your brow. Never write another line nor raise a fist to any man." His words and his music are like Christmas morning. I go forth, a seer.

The Yogurt of Vasirin Kefirovsky

Vasirin Kefirovsky stands six feet four and uses an extra-long rubber-tipped pointer. He is fond of spinning a globe with this pointer while his feet rest on the patio table. He dislikes gossip but revels in small talk. His wife, Emily, spends many of her mornings watching the yogurt incubate beneath blankets in her stainless-steel kitchen. Dr. Kefirovsky spins his globe and thinks from eight to eleven forty-five, then he drinks his yogurt and works all afternoon on *Earth Story*.

Today his morning schedule is interrupted by an interviewer from *Time* magazine, Robert Williams, assistant science editor.

Mrs. Kefirovsky sits with the two men at the patio table, keeping her eye on the weather. She sips a cocktail of Mogen David wine and club soda.

"I am what I am," says Professor Kefirovsky. "When I was a boy, I ate wide noodles brushed with cheeses. In middle age, no meat was too gamy. I ate your turtles, your rabbits, your unfit leghorns. I knew the earth before I knew my own belly."

"Your husband is a great man," the reporter tells Emily. "If the deep space probes bear out his ideas as well as Mariner II did, he'll be on the cover of *Time* someday. He'll be taught in the schools."

Kefirovsky puts down his pointer and uses a long forefinger for emphasis. "Eating has nothing to do with thinking," he tells the reporter. "I always thought clearly, but I thought too much about food. Now I think about nothing to eat. What is yogurt?

It's milk and time and heat. What is the earth? It's rocks and time and bodies."

The reporter takes notes slowly. "But tell me this, Professor, have you resented being an outsider all these years? I mean, has the fact that the scientific community considers you something of a charlatan embittered your career?"

Kefirovsky spins the earth with his pointer. "Name me a big one who was not an outsider. Galileo, Copernicus, Paracelsus, Hans Fricht . . . Galen maybe was an insider, he gave back rubs to the Emperor. He was a chiropractor. If you're an insider you make Vicks cough drops or you work for the Ford Foundation."

"Well, Einstein, for one, was accepted by his contemporaries. He was not an outsider."

Kefirovsky stands and edges the pointer close to Williams' nose. "And Einstein made cough drops too. Only if you write this everyone will say how ungrateful Kefirovsky is. Now that people pay attention to him, he fills the magazines with dreck about Einstein. Not long ago I saw Einstein's brain. It's in Connecticut at a health institute. They take care of it like it's a member of the family in an iron lung. I knew Einstein and I knew his brother Victor, who sold Red Ball shoes in Brooklyn."

"Don't worry, Professor, *Time* isn't a gossip magazine. I won't write anything about Einstein."

"I don't worry and I don't think about eating food." Using his pointer as a walking stick, Kefirovsky strides into his garden bordered by petunias, roses, and white azaleas. The reporter follows.

"I came from Russia in a dressing gown. At Ellis Island I cut it below the pockets with a scissors, hemmed the bottom, and wore it for years as a satin smoking jacket. I had my teeth capped during World War II. I married in 1926 and have four sons all of whom served in the United States Army and were honorably discharged, except Gerald."

"And what does Gerald do now?"

"He makes cough drops."

Mrs. Kefirovsky returns to the kitchen with her candy thermometer to check the yogurt's temperature. "I'll call you, Vasi, when it's a hundred and twelve."

Dr. Kefirovsky is neither tired nor angry. He suffers the reporter but his mind is elsewhere. His four sons are all organic chemists. They used to come together every year at Easter time and eat big meals of lake trout, poultry, beef, and Russian side dishes like stuffed cabbage, boiled potatoes, and fried smelt. Kefirovsky himself used to make two hundred gallons of wine a year. During the Christmas season neighbors and delivery men drank it from Pepsi-Cola quarts.

There are two ovens in his stainless-steel kitchen and a natural-gas pit-barbecue in his backyard. But Kefirovsky no longer cooks, barbecues, or makes wine. His sons and their families are refusing to come for another Easter. The mailman and the paperboy turn down the quarts of Christmas yogurt. The books he wrote thirty years ago about the collisions of the planets are selling now, but his new thesis is scorned by people like Adelle Davis and Dr. Atkins. He has no publisher for *Earth Story*.

Williams asks, "When did you first begin to realize that cosmic accidents are recorded in human history?"

"I knew this as early as 1929."

"But what made you think of it?"

"I opened my eyes. I looked around. I talked to people. I read books. I wondered why a rinky-dinky town like Troy should be such a front-page story for a thousand years. I wondered why the Red Sea opened and how come the Chinamen knew about Noah's flood. I kept my eyes on the heavens. I read spectrograms. I made educated guesses. That's what science is.

"One day I came to Hans Fricht and I said, 'Hans, either I'm crazy or I know about history.' I showed him my data. 'You're not crazy,' he said. He called Einstein, who was then a nobody, a refugee in baggy trousers who thanked God when you talked to him in German and had hay fever in New Jersey.

" '*Er veiss vas er zagt?*' Einstein asked Fricht. He followed the mathematics but he missed the point. He didn't give a damn about history. Before he died he was a pen pal with Albert Schweitzer. I sent Schweitzer a copy of *Worlds in Confusion* but never heard from him. Fricht was going to write the introduction but he said Einstein needed the money, so Einstein wrote it in German and Hans translated it. Einstein had lots of bad grammar. Listen, I liked the man. I am not jealous of his success. He was right about many things. If he ate less, he would be alive today."

Emily Kefirovsky comes out the back door and down the two wooden steps to the patio. She approaches the flower garden carrying a blue cardigan over her forearm. "Vasi, the sun is behind the clouds. Here." She hands him the cardigan. "He's not a young man, Mr. Williams, although the cold never bothers him. During the winters in Berlin, even in Moscow, he never wore gloves. Here in Texas you can't tell from one minute to the next. The air conditioning makes him dizzy. I wish we could move."

Kefirovsky puts on the cardigan. "Go watch the yogurt," he tells her. "It will be ready to pour in a few minutes." He strokes the sweater to be certain it is just right. With his pointer he marks the spot where Emily stood. "My wife eats saturated fats. Look at yourself. Probably not forty and I'll bet your veins are closing up like artichokes."

"Maybe you're right, Professor Kefirovsky, but let's finish talking about you. I'm not important. I'm just an anonymous pencil at *Time*, but you're a famous man. Whether scientists like it or not your works are right up there in general sales, right up there with Dr. Spock and Dr. Rubin and Dr. Atkins."

"These are kids' stuff. Not just Spock, the other ones too. I've read all the diet books. Atkins is what they used to call a piss prophet. They ran them out of town in Germany. They would set up fairs and sell medicine like hucksters. They sent you to the toilet with litmus paper and when they read the colors they sold you their medicine. That's what Atkins is. And Rubin, he doesn't even know what Wilhelm Reich knew."

"Did you know Wilhelm Reich?"

"I knew him in the days before he made the boxes. He used to come over too, to talk to me like Eidler and Fricht and the others. He liked cold asparagus dipped in mayonnaise. He never drank beer. If they hadn't tortured him in California, I believe he would be alive today."

Kefirovsky leads the reporter, single file, through his garden along a circular path. Behind the flowers are green plants and shrubs, some in blossom. In the deep shade there are patches of soft dark moss. The professor points at various plants but does not describe them. "I am not a botanist. Pliny the Elder classified plants and Hippocrates' son-in-law classified people. There are many plants that can kill you but not a one that will eat you. I was an old man before I thought of this."

"Is that so significant?" The reporter has put away his ball point. His hands are clasped behind his back, the notebook sticks out of his pocket. He looks bored. From the kitchen Mrs. Kefirovsky calls out, "A hundred and eleven point eight." The Professor walks briskly toward the house. "After one hundred and ten we switch from the candy thermometer to the new digital types that give you an exact reading."

In the stainless-steel kitchen sink he washes his hands with green liquid soap and dries them carefully on a paper towel. The yogurt is in a three-quart glass jar immersed in water within a very deep electric frying pan. The digital thermometer lies in the yogurt just as snugly as if the mixture were a patient's milky tongue. Kefirovsky takes a plastic container from the refrigerator and spoons a sticky material into the yogurt. The aroma is strong and brisk, it smells almost like wintergreen.

"What's that?" Williams asks.

Mrs. Kefirovsky looks surprised. "He didn't tell you yet?"

"No, but I will," the Professor says. "Now we must wait for at least fifteen minutes while the entire mixture resonates at one hundred and twelve degrees Fahrenheit. Then we pour it into pints, where it can stay for almost a week. The store yogurts are good for two months or more. Mine is not the same. This is good for six days only."

Mrs. Kefirovsky sits on a stool, her heavy legs dangling playfully. The reporter and the Professor are on chrome-and-vinyl kitchen chairs facing the yogurt. Kefirovsky has again taken up his pointer. "What I added to the yogurt is a sticky sweet extract of an Arabic plant called 'mahn,' spelled m-a-n. I imported it from Saudi Arabia, Egypt, and Morocco. The Moroccan one grows best here. I harvest it and freeze it. It's also good for the breath like chlorophyll gum.

"Fifteen years ago all you heard was chlorophyll. Then everyone got interested in outer space and transistors. I am the opposite. I started with space forty, fifty years ago, and now I'm back to chlorophyll. Science is like that. We are always breaking up substances to look for the soul of the material. My sons, the chemists, don't know this. They just do jobs for the oil companies."

"Not everyone is an original thinker like you, Vasi," Mrs. Kefirovsky states from her high position on the stool. "Mr. Williams, don't get the wrong impression about the boys. They're good chemists. But Vasi has no patience for people who learn to do something and then do it. He learns something and then he does something else."

"That's what science is," the Professor says.

"Twelve minutes, Vasi." Mrs. Kefirovsky watches the kitchen clock from her perch.

"I started thinking about this only a few years ago, after Hans Fricht died. He was the last of my colleagues. I noticed how all of us pallbearers could hardly carry him. I thought, We're just too old for such work. But that wasn't it. Hans Fricht, whom I loved like a brother, ate too much."

"He did," Emily adds. "He liked to eat small meals every hour while he worked."

"This started me thinking altogether about eating. Then I went to the old books, the way I did after I studied physics and astronomy. I thought to myself, if the heavens got into these books, why not the foods? So I read all the Greeks, mostly Homer, who is full of eating. I kept tables on who ate what, anybody I could find. Achilles lived on fifteen hundred calories a day and drank enough wine to die of cirrhosis by the time he was twenty-two. Priam had a hundred sons, yet Troy was only as big as a fooball field. Their food came in wagons from the east of the city because the Greeks never cut off their supplies. The Trojan horse is really a story about death from a full belly, but this is not the evidence I sought. I didn't want to interpret the books, I wanted the evidence right there in black and white for anyone to see."

"He didn't want people to say, 'Oh, there goes Kefirovsky

again,' " says Emily. "He wanted it to be exact. Ten minutes, Vasi."

"So I kept reading the myths, the Upanishads, the Book of the Dead, the I Ching, until I found it right before my eyes."

"Where?" Williams asks, although he makes no attempt to take notes.

"Exodus. Right there in Exodus. This served me right for not checking earlier. But outside of the Flood I had never found very much decent natural history there. Anyway, that's where it was, Exodus 16:13. Have you heard of manna, 'manna from heaven'?"

"Do you mean what the Israelites ate in the desert?"

"Don't call them 'Israelites,' you make them sound like flashlights. They were no kind of 'ites.' The Egyptians called them Abirus. And they weren't in the desert. The best evidence is that the Sinai peninsula was in partial bloom at the time, enough to sustain nomads if they went, now and then, into Canaan or Egypt for grain."

"Well, forgive me, Professor, I'm only a layman."

"You make that sound like 'amen.' " Kefirovsky laughs. "The flashlights said 'amen' in the desert." He stands and walks over to the yogurt surrounded by simmering water.

"Still eight minutes," Emily calls out.

The Professor jabs his pointer at Williams' white patent shoe and looks the reporter in the eye. "I know what the flashlights ate."

"Yogurt?"

Kefirovsky goes to the window and grins out at his rose garden. "In Exodus they call it 'a fine flakelike thing like hoarfrost on the ground.' They say it tasted like wafers made with honey."

"Vasi lets me put a little honey in his, it's the only sweet he uses and it's because of that passage that he lets me do it. Six minutes."

"Do you know what they call yogurt now in the Middle East, where it is a staple?"

Williams says he does not know.

"They call it *Leben*. This means 'life' in German. And that

Moroccan plant whose sweet milk is thick as motor oil, the Arabs call that one *man*. Do you see what hangs on in language? Man and life. Plain as the nose on your face. Once you know it, it's all over the Bible. 'Man does not live by bread alone' is only half a sentence."

"Wait a minute, Professor, I'm not sure I follow this. The linguistic hints are one thing, but how could yogurt appear in the desert?"

"You ask questions just like Herman Eidler asked. Right away to the first cause. Well, I don't know how yogurt appeared to the Abirus. That's for the theologians. I am a scientist. Science is two things, a problem and a guess. The earth is rocks and organisms decaying together at a fixed rate and under uniform pressure. In Exodus it says that this flakelike stuff melted when the sun grew hot. I don't know. I don't sell cough drops. But I can tell you this, the recipe has been before our eyes for a few thousand years and nobody has read it. They all say, look what the flashlights gave us, ethics, morals, ten commandments. But everybody else gave us the commandments too. Every priest in Egypt, every Hindu, every Parsee, every Chaldean, every Hammurabi, even the African cannibals roasting children had do's and do nots. We read the Bible but we missed the recipes."

"Four minutes, Vasi." Mrs. Kefirovsky slides off the stool. Beyond the stainless-steel kitchen she disappears amid the dark wood furnishings of other rooms. "I'll be back in time," she says as her voice trails away.

Kefirovsky stares at his yogurt. The digital thermometer reads a constant one hundred and twelve degrees. "Pretty soon we'll pour and when it cools you can have some. If I'd been making this thirty years ago, my friends might still be here. We used to meet on most Sundays just to joke about things. Herman Eidler would come and Hans Fricht, of course, and Jerome Van Strung. Sometimes Einstein came over from Princeton. You would call us a think tank. They were just a bunch of krauts smacking their lips over wurst and sauerbraten. We worried about the war. Eidler lost his whole family and his wife's family. Van Strung had letters from Walter Benjamin that nobody else ever saw.

They all liked to play croquet on my lawn. Sometimes I read sections from *Worlds in Confusion* out loud while they swung their mallets. Fricht was a beekeeper and clean as a Band-Aid. Einstein and Van Strung could walk barefoot over the dogshit.

"And after croquet it was food and beer. All the time, Einstein knew about the bomb and ate heavy meals. He never talked about his work. I naturally did and Fricht talked about his bees and Van Strung talked literature. When the war was over, Eidler brought us, one Sunday, three dozen Nathan's hot dogs straight from Coney Island in an ice chest. He came in a government car with a chauffeur. He brought them with buns and everything, but the ice melted onto the bread. Emily rewarmed the hot dogs and we ate them plain. That was the way we celebrated VE day. We ate and we talked.

"There is a former football player in California who writes to me. He eats only on the weekends and has done this since he retired as a defensive player four years ago. He knows many people in California who survive on nuts and figs. We are doing metabolism and blood tests on him and keeping data. In the summer he runs a camp for overweight boys. Parents bring their sons there just to watch a man not eat and be cheerful and busy all week."

"Vasi, it's fifteen minutes." Emily reappears with a large funnel and a photo album. Dr. Kefirovsky removes the thermometer, puts on two stove mittens, and lifting the big glass container out of the boiling water, pours his yogurt into the funnel above the small glass containers which will house the mixture.

"It's not ready yet," Emily says, "still lumpy." Kefirovsky pours the pint of liquid back into the three-quart jar. "We'll have to wait a few minutes more for the *man* to melt. It happens sometimes because it doesn't freeze uniformly. It doesn't hurt anything."

"We would do this once a week if it was just for Vasi," Emily says. "But we make it most days to give to others. All the neighbors get some and we mail throughout the area in winter when the spoilage rate is low."

"You mail it in glass containers?" the reporter asks.

"No, we mail it in plastic with tight lids. It can go about three days without refrigeration when it's fresh. Most of them probably don't even taste it. In '72 we mailed one to Nixon and one to McGovern special delivery. Not even a thank you from either one. A few people have heard about it and come to ask for some."

"Have you ever tried to sell it?"

"He talks like Gerald," Kefirovsky says, and walks back out to the garden still wearing his oven mittens.

"I didn't mean to offend him," the reporter says to Emily.

"It's all right. He's sensitive because Gerald, actually all of the boys, stand up to him." She opens the photo album to what seem to be recent Polaroid snapshots of healthy middle-aged men and women surrounded by children. "We have wonderful sons and grandchildren. They respect their father too, and they wouldn't try to stop him from doing whatever he wants to do. But they won't allow me to be on the yogurt diet. Don't get me wrong, I like it and believe Vasi is discovering scientific truths, but I eat it and I'm still hungry. Gerald ships me cornfed beef from Iowa. I have to send a photograph every month to prove to him that I'm not losing weight like their father. Vasi used to weigh over two twenty, now, you can see for yourself he's a string bean. The doctors say he's healthy, but he should take vitamins. Since he's been growing *man* down here, he's eaten nothing but the yogurt and *man*. We moved here from New Jersey when he realized Texas was the right climate for the *man*. We tried Florida and California first, and he ate other food there because he admits that yogurt without *man* isn't enough. The boys told him to sell the recipe, but he wants to get the book out first, *Earth Story*, to explain all about it. Otherwise it would just be another food product.

"I hope you understand that with Vasi there is no halfway. He is his own laboratory. The boys know this. Gerald says, 'One laboratory is enough for him. Let him starve himself, but if I catch him forcing you to live on that stuff, I'll break his bony back.' That's why he won't speak to Gerald. But Gerald loves him. All the boys do and the grandchildren too. You can't just make a whole family, twelve grandchildren and all, stop eating everything but yogurt and *man*.

"It's one thing to have a theory about history. The boys backed him one hundred percent on that. And it wasn't easy. Here they were studying to be scientists and all the famous scientists saying their father was a fraud. Gerald quit one chemistry class because of something the teacher said about Vasi. The boys think he might be right about the yogurt too, but they don't want him to starve me and to starve their families. That's not wrong, is it? Did Pasteur give his kids TB or Salk carry around polio?"

"It's not the same." Dr. Kefirovsky is back in the kitchen carrying a fresh sprig of the *man* plant. "I wear these mittens because the plant is full of stickers. I'm just showing you a sprig. Outside, we milk it like the maple trees in Vermont."

"Is it a lot like maple syrup?" the reporter asks.

"Much thicker in texture. It freezes slowly and looks like peanut brittle when I put it in the yogurt."

Williams feels his pocket to make sure the notebook is there. He uncrosses his legs and seems ready to leave.

"I'm afraid, Dr. Kefirovsky, that I really don't follow all of this. Don't get me wrong, I appreciate your showing me exactly how you make this yogurt even though I'm here to talk about your earlier work. What I don't see is the jump from your discovery that yogurt is Old Testament manna, to the point of excluding all other food. I mean the . . . flashlights ate other food too, didn't they?"

"Not for forty years. For forty years they lived on this and then, only then, were they ready to pick up the business of destiny. This was a time out in history, just like during a football game. This is built into the organism. In sleep, in a nervous breakdown, in menopause, the body is always saying 'time out.' Social organizations too. Governments. There is the New Deal and then an Eisenhower. The Revolution and then Stalin. Going out of Egypt, then forty years in the desert. That was the only time they did it right.

"Imagine if in 1922 we Russians had sat down on the steppes, sat down in our cities, sat down by the Black Sea, in the Urals, in Siberia, all over, Russians sitting down saying to each other, 'Time out. Congratulations on the revolution, now let's have a time out for forty years to eat *man* and yogurt.' Would there have been Stalinism? Would the people swill vodka and be fat as pigs? There are two things to learn from Exodus. Take time out and eat the right thing."

"So you think everyone in the world should at least temporarily go on this diet?"

"First they should have their teeth pulled."

Emily laughs, showing hers. "The boys never even took you seriously on that, Vasi." Kefirovsky opens his mouth and with his forefinger goes in a circle pushing his upper lip and then his lower lip away from his empty gums.

"I hadn't noticed," the reporter says.

"Exactly, it doesn't matter. I happen to have lost mine nine years ago from pyorrhea. When I learned what I now know, I gave away the false ones. Teeth are an evolutionary accident. There is no doubt that we're losing them faster than chest hair. We needed them only until the domestication of animals. For six or seven thousand years teeth have been an anachronism."

"To whom did you give your false teeth? I find that pretty unusual."

"To the Illinois College of Optometry. They have all the manuscripts. I went there in 1927."

"That's news to me. I don't recall that in your biographical profile."

"I didn't stay for a degree. At the time Hans Fricht was a professor of optics there. I knew little English. A Russian astronomer was not needed anywhere. Hans said to me, 'Become an eye doctor, there is nothing to it.' He got me a scholarship. It was the first place in this country where we lived. Later I went to New Jersey. The optometry trustees asked for my notebooks and my old eyeglasses. In 1965 they made a Kefirovsky room. In 1973 I sent my teeth also."

Kefirovsky checks the mixture. "Five minutes more should do it. The only thing I'm not sure of is the forty years. I don't know if the time out has to be that long or if it can be shortened. Do you think you could eat this for forty years?"

"Exclusively?"

"Exclusively."

"I don't think so, Professor, at least I wouldn't want to try."

"I am seventy-seven years old. In order for me to try it forty years I would have to live to be one hundred and sixteen. This is possible, but unlikely. There will perhaps be no other scientist to follow in my footsteps. Science will produce more Corfam and SST engines. The keys to natural history lay shrouded for thousands of years, now we refuse to see the one true gift of the gods. Easy, abundant, tasty, and wrapped in a time out. If the clergymen would wake up, they would see it. What is the promised land? Milk and honey and time. What is yogurt? Milk and bacteria and time. Why did the people who lived on manna for forty years want a land of milk and honey? Why not a land of pomegranates? Why not a land of barley and sesame seed and olive oil? Why not wine and cheese? Where else do you read about milk and honey? Nowhere. I've looked. And what sort of honey would you find in a semiarid climate where the annual rainfall could hardly support a large bee population. If Hans Fricht was alive, he would be an immense help now. He knew bees from A to Z. He would have seen immediately. He used to say, 'Where the bee sucks, there suck I,' and Eidler and Van Strung would laugh at him saying that while he hit the croquet ball and jumped up and down when he had a clean blocking shot. He knew the bee signal language before anybody wrote about it. Hans could have understood birds too if he would have tried. We all worshiped that man. Einstein brought him page after page of dull formulas by the thousands until one day Hans said to him, 'This is it, you *glücklich* kraut. You've finally got something worthwhile here.' And that's the only time he ever praised Einstein. But it's once more than he praised me. He used to say to me, 'Vasi, lay off, they're not ready for you. Try a hobby.' When I left optometry college, he thought I should be a pharmacist. But I was lucky, I got a job at the Institute. Hans himself was unemployed for twenty-two years. They made him leave the optometry faculty when they found out he was not an optometrist. After that he was a sponge, a hanger-on, a misfit. Imagine such a misfit. He wouldn't take a penny from anyone.

He was an expert sewer and knitter. One of the great minds of the twentieth century making his own suits and sweaters. He raised his own vegetables. The man lived on a few hundred dollars a year. His friends made sure he had plenty to eat and that was our mistake. We tried to be generous and our butterball turkeys, our triscuits, our dark beer, and our wurst, all this killed him."

Kefirovsky is almost breathless. He leans on his pointer and his body shakes with sobs.

"Vasi loved Hans Fricht," Emily says. "You would have too. There was a scientist and a human being. Godfather to all the boys."

"It's a shame that he had such a hard life," the reporter says. "I've actually never heard of him."

"That is science," says Kefirovsky.

"If Hans was alive," Emily adds, "he wouldn't let you starve yourself like this. That's why you're so weak that you can hardly talk for a few minutes. You're the thinker, let someone else starve to prove you're right. Thousands of college students are looking for jobs like this. They swallow goldfish and squeeze into telephone booths and now they kiss for two weeks at a time. These people could prove you're right and you could live to see it. Ask the reporter."

"She has a point, Professor. Lots of students do paid experiments. But I don't want to get into the midst of a family squabble about this."

"Look at him," Emily screams, "look at him. How can you say you don't want to mix in? You've listened to a brilliant scientist talk, don't you want to save his life?"

Kefirovsky remains calm. He smiles at the reporter and raising his pointer directs the rubber tip at his wife. "She means well, but in spite of my many explanations Emily does not see that it is the yogurt that keeps me alive and well. At my age the average man has been dead for seven years."

"From two hundred and ten pounds to one-forty-five, that's how it's keeping you alive." She addresses the reporter. "Write this in *Time* magazine, that he can't walk stairs, that I have to tie his shoes. He's dizzy from air conditioning, and he chokes on the heat. He sits at his desk and starves himself. For two years I've watched. Enough is enough."

Still smiling, Kefirovsky says, "The revolution that is coming will make you forget Marx. Eating three meals will be like having three wives. Ordinary people by the millions will have their teeth pulled and drink happily ever after. Science and scarcity change the world. The yogurt will end scarcity, another time out is coming. You'll see. Marx and Malthus will be as forgotten as Paracelsus and Agrippa. Do you know what they worried about? Thousands of years ago Heraclitus, a smart man, thought the earth was packed tight as a suitcase. Everyone is wrong. Someday I'll be wrong too. That is science. In the meantime, it's time out. The Babylonians were a thin people but the Philistines gorged themselves. Huns were thinner than Romans. It's the law of history. Look at the Ethiopians. Look at the black Africans who weigh eighty pounds and can chase a giraffe for three days without food or water."

"It's terrible to watch." From her seat on the kitchen stool, Emily sobs and watches the kitchen clock. "The five minutes are up, Vasi." Emily wipes her eyes and once more raises the funnel. The Professor takes up his mittens and approaches the calm yogurt in the midst of bubbling waters. "This time it's good and ready." He holds the heavy glass jar steadily, the blue veins in his forearms stretch and tremble with the exercise, but Kefirovsky's pouring hand is still and even. Expertly, Emily moves the funnel from one pint bottle to the next, spilling only droplets on the stainless-steel counter. As coordinated as a ballet, their hands move the thick milky liquid over and into its bottles in a silent rhythmical pattern. As the big jar becomes lighter, the Professor does not quicken the pace of his pouring nor does Emily speed the funnel. The yogurt drops like long thick tongues into the bottles and it stops at the very tip of each one without overflowing. It bubbles for a second and then expires. With thick corks Emily seals ten bottles while Kefirovsky and the reporter watch her strong fingers. She leaves two unsealed. Kefirovsky pours his yogurt into a yellow glass decorated with the figures of parrots. "Do you want to drink yours or eat it with a spoon?" he asks the reporter.

"I'll drink," Williams says. "Isn't Mrs. Kefirovsky having any?"

"No," she says, "I have a steak in the broiler. I usually drink one at night while Vasi is reading."

The Professor raises his glass. A slight steam rises from the yogurt. With the gesture of a toast he extends his glass toward Emily, who stands in front of the ten corked bottles. Her eyes are vaguely red, and in the silent kitchen the noise of a broiling steak begins to be heard. Emily nods and smiles at Kefirovsky, who then makes the same gesture to the reporter. "To science," Emily says as the two men slowly raise to their lips the white flakelike liquid, thick as dew and fine as the hoarfrost on the ground.

Understanding Alvarado

I

Castro thought it was no accident that Achilles "Archie" Alvarado held the world record for being hit in the head by a pitched ball.

"Because he was a hero even then," Fidel said, "because he stood like a hero with his neck proudly over the plate."

When people asked Mrs. Alvarado what she thought of her husband's career, she said, "Chisox okay, the rest of the league stinks. Archie, he liked to play every day, bench him and his knees ached, his fingers swelled, his tongue forgot English. He would say, 'Estelle, let's split, let's scram, *vámonos a* Cuba. What we owe to Chisox?'

"I'd calm him down. 'Arch,' I'd say, 'Arch, Chisox have been plenty good to us. Paid five gees more than Tribe, first-class hotels, white roomies on the road, good press.'

" 'Estelle,' he would say, 'I can't take it no more. They got me down to clubbing in the pinch and only against southpaws. They cut Chico Carasquel and Sammy Esposito and Cactus Bob Kuzava. What we owe to Chisox?'

"When it got like that, I would say, 'Talk to Zloto,' and Zloto would say, 'Man, you Latinos sure are hotheads. I once got nine hits in a row for the Birds, was Rookie of the Year for the Bosox. I have the largest hands in either league and what do you think I do? I sit on the bench and spit-shine my street shoes. Look there, you can see your greasy black mug in 'em.' Zloto always knew how to handle Alvarado."

Zloto came to Havana, showed Fidel his hands, talked about the '50s. Fidel said, "They took our good men and put them in Yankee uniforms, in Bosox, Chisox, Dodgers, Birds. They took our manhood, Zloto. They took our Achilles and called him Archie. Hector Gonzalez they called Ramrod, Jesús Ortiz they made a Jayo. They treated Cuban manhood like a bowl of chicos and ricos. Yes, we have no bananas but we got vine-ripened Latinos who play good ball all year, stick their heads over the plate, and wait for the Revolution. Fidel Castro gave it to them. It was three and two on me in Camagüey around November 1960. There were less than two dozen of us. Batista had all roads blocked and there was hardly enough ammunition left to kill some rabbits. He could have starved us out but he got greedy, he wanted the quick inning. When I saw that he was coming in with his best stuff with his dark one out over the middle, I said to Che and to Francisco Muñiz, 'Habana for Christmas,' and I lined his fascist pitch up his capitalist ass."

"I'm not impressed," Zloto said. "When I heard about the Bay of Pigs I said to myself, 'Let's wipe those oinks right off the face of the earth.' You took Cuba, our best farm property, and went Commie with it. You took our best arms, Castro, our speed- and our curve-ball artists. You dried up our Cuban diamonds."

"Zloto, Zloto," Fidel said. "Look at this picture of your buddy, 'Archie' Alvarado. Don't you like him better as 'Achilles'? Look at his uniform, look at his AK 47 rifle."

"I liked him better when he was number twenty-three and used a thirty-six-inch Hillerich and Bradsby Louisville Slugger to pound out line drives in Comiskey Park."

"There's no more Comiskey Park," Fidel said. "No more Grace, no more Chuck Comiskey to come down after a tough extra-inning loss and buy a drink for the whole clubhouse. No more free Bulova watches. The Chisox are run by an insurance company now. You punch a time clock before batting practice and they charge for overtime in the whirlpool bath."

"That's goddamn pinko propaganda," Zloto said.

"You've been outta the game, big Victor," Fidel said. "You've been sitting too long out in Arizona being a dental assistant. You haven't been on the old diamonds, now AstroTurfed, closed to the sun, and air-conditioned. You have not seen the bleachers go to two-fifty. While you've been in Arizona the world changed, Zloto. Look at our Achilles, four fractured skulls, thirteen years in the big time. Played all over the outfield, played first and played third. A lifetime mark of two ninety-nine and RBIs in the thousands. He never got an Achilles day from Chisox, Bosox, Tribe, or Birds. When he came home Fidel made him a day, made him a reservist colonel. I did this because Achilles Alvarado is not chickenshit. You, Zloto, know this better than anyone.

"Achilles said to me the first time we met, 'Fidel, the big time is over for Archie Alvarado, but send me to the cane fields, give me a machete, and I'll prove that Alvarado has enough arm left to do something for Cuba.' A hero, this Achilles 'Archie' Alvarado, but they sent him back to us a broken-down, used-up pinch hitter with no eye, no arm, and no speed.

" 'Achilles, Archie,' I said, 'the Revolution was not made for Chisox, Bosox, Bengals, and Birds. We didn't take Habana for chicos and ricos. Cuba Libre doesn't give a flying fuck for RBIs. The clutch hit is every minute here, baby brother. Cuba loves you for your Cuban heart. I'll make you a colonel, a starter in the only game that counts. Your batting average will be counted in lives saved, in people educated, fed, and protected from capitalist exploitation.' "

"Cut the shit, Fidel," Zloto said. "I'm here because Archie will be eligible for his pension in September. He'll pull in a thousand a month for the rest of his days. That'll buy a lot of bananas down here, won't it?

"You may think that you understand Alvarado, Fidel, but I knew the man for eight years, roomed with him on the Chisox and the Bosox. I've seen him high, seen him in slumps you wouldn't believe. I've seen him in the dugout after being picked off first in a crucial situation. You wouldn't know what that's like, Castro. I'm talking about a man who has just met a fast ball and stroked it over the infield. He has made the wide turn at first and watched the resin of his footprint settle around the bag.

He has thrown off the batting helmet and pulled the soft, long-billed cap from his hip pocket. The coach has slapped his ass and twenty, thirty, maybe forty thousand Chisox fans start stomping their feet while the organ plays 'Charge,' and then he is picked off in a flash, caught scratching his crotch a foot from the bag. And it's all over. You hear eighty thousand feet stop stomping. The first baseman snickers behind his glove; even the ump smiles. I've seen Alvarado at times like that cry like a baby. He'd throw a towel over his head and say, 'Zloto, I'm a no-good dummy. Good hit and no head. We coulda won it all here in the top of the ninth. That Yankee pitcher is good for shit. My dumb-ass move ruined the Chisox chances.' He would sit in front of his locker taking it real hard until the GM or even Chuck Comiskey himself would come down and say, 'Archie, it's just one game that you blew with a dumb move. We're still in it, still in the thick of the race. You'll help these Sox plenty during the rest of the year. Now take your shower and get your ass over to a Mexican restaurant.' The Alvarado that I knew, Castro, that Alvarado could come back the next afternoon, sometimes the next inning, and change the complexion of a game."

Fidel laughed and lit a cigar. "Zloto, you've been away too long. The Archie you knew, this man went out of style with saddle shoes and hula hoops. Since the days you're talking about when Alvarado cried over a pick-off play, since then Che and Muñiz are dead and two Kennedys assassinated. There have been wars in the Far East and Middle East and in Bangladesh. There have been campus shootings, a revolution of the Red Guard, an ouster of Khrushchev, a fascist massacre in Indonesia, two revolutions in Uruguay, fourteen additions to the U.N. There has been détente and Watergate and a Washington-Peking understanding and where have you been, Zloto? You've been in Tucson, Arizona, reading the newspaper on Sunday and cleaning teeth. Even dental techniques have changed. Look at your fluorides and your gum brushing method."

"All right, boys," Mrs. Alvarado said, "enough is enough. What are we going to prove anyway by reminiscing about the good old days? Zloto means well. He came here as a friend. Twelve grand a year for life is not small potatoes to Archie and me. In the Windy City or in Beantown we could live in a nice integrated neighborhood on that kind of money and pick up a little extra by giving autographs at Chevy dealerships. Fidel, you know that Archie always wanted to stay in the game. In one interview he told Bill Fuller of the *Sun-Times* that he wanted to manage the Chisox someday. They didn't want any black Cuban managers in the American League, not then. But, like you say, Fidel, a lot of water has gone under the bridge since those last days when Archie was catching slivers for the Bosox, Chisox, and Birds. These days, there might even be some kind of front-office job to round off that pension. Who knows, it might be more than he made twenty years ago when he led the league in RBIs."

Castro said, "Estelle, apart from all ideological arguments, you are just dreaming. Achilles was never a U.S. citizen. After a dozen years as one of Castro's colonels, do you really think Uncle Sam is going to say, 'Cm'on up here, Archie, take a front-office job and rake in the cash'? Do you really think America works that way, Estelle? I know Zloto thinks that, but you've been down here all this time, don't you understand capitalist exploitation by now?"

Estelle said, "Fidel, I'm not saying that we are going to give up the ideals of the Revolution and I'm not deluded by the easy capitalist life. I am thinking about only getting what's coming to us. Alvarado put in the time, he should get the pension."

"That's the whole reason I took a week off to come down here," Zloto said. "The commissioner called me up—he heard we were buddies—and said, 'Zloto, you might be in a position to do your old friend Alvarado some good, that is if you're willing to travel.' The commissioner absolutely guaranteed that Archie would get his pension if he came back up and established residence. The commissioner of baseball is not about to start mailing monthly checks through the Swiss embassy, and I don't blame him. The commissioner is not even saying you have to stay permanently in the U.S. He is just saying, 'Come up, get an apartment, make a few guest appearances, an interview or two, and then do whatever the hell you want.' "

Fidel said, "Yes, go up to America and tell them how mean Fidel is, how bad the sugar crop was, and how poor and hungry we Cubans are. Tell them what they want to hear and they'll pension you off. The Achilles I know would swallow poison before he'd kowtow to the memory of John Foster Dulles that way. They sent an Archie back home, but Cuba Libre reminded him he was really an Achilles."

"Fidel, let's not get sentimental," Mrs. Alvarado said. "Let's talk turkey. We want the twelve grand a year, right?"

"Right, but only because it is the fruit of Achilles' own labor."

"Okay, in order to get the money we have to go back."

"I could take it up in the United Nations, I could put the pressure on. Kissinger is very shaky in Latin America. He knows we all know that he doesn't give a fuck about any country except Venezuela. I could do it through Waldheim, and nobody would have to know. Then we could threaten to go public if they hold out on what's coming to him."

Zloto said, "America doesn't hold out on anybody, Castro. Ask Joe Stalin's daughter if you don't believe me. You guys are batting your heads against the wall by hating us. There's nothing to hate. We want a square deal for everyone. In this case too. As for Kissinger, he might carry some weight with the Arabs, but the commissioner of baseball cannot be pressured. That damned fool Alvarado should have become a citizen while he was playing in the States. I didn't know he wasn't a citizen. It was just crazy not to become one. Every other Latin does."

"But our Achilles, he was always different," Castro said. "He always knew that the Chisox, Bosox, Birds, and Braves didn't own the real thing. The real Achilles Alvarado was in Camagüey with me, in Bolivia with Che, with Mao on the Long March."

"The real Achilles was just too lazy to do things right," Mrs. Alvarado said. "He didn't want to fill out complicated papers, so he stayed an alien. As long as he had a job, it didn't matter."

"Zloto," Fidel said, "you one-time Rookie of the Year, now a fat, tooth-cleaning capitalist, you want to settle this the way Achilles would settle this? I mean why should we bring in Kissinger and Waldheim and everyone else? I say if a man believes

in the Revolution, what's a pension to him? You think I couldn't
have been a Wall Street lawyer? And what about our Doctor
Che? You don't think he would have made a big pension in the
AMA? I say our Achilles has recovered his Cuban manhood. He
won't want to go back. Estelle does not speak for him."

"Fidel is right," she said. "I do not speak for Archie Alvarado,
I only write his English for him."

"If Estelle wants to go back and be exploited, let her go. Do
you want those television announcers calling you Mrs. Archie
again as if you had stepped from the squares of a comic strip?
Does the wife of a colonel in the Cuban Army sound like a
comic-strip girl to you, Zloto?"

"Fidel," Estelle said, "don't forget the issue is not so large.
Only a trip to the Windy City or Beantown, maybe less than
two weeks in all."

"You are forgetting," Fidel said, "what happened to Kid Gavilan when he went back to see an eye surgeon in New York. They
put his picture in *Sepia* and in the *National Enquirer*, the news
services showed him with his bulging eye being hugged by a
smooth-faced Sugar Ray Robinson. They wanted it to seem like
this: here are two retired Negro fighters. One is a tap dancer
in Las Vegas, the other has for ten years been working in the
cane fields of Castro's Cuba. Look at how healthy the American
Negro is. His teeth are white as ever, his step lithe in Stetson
shoes, while our Kid Gavilan, once of the bolo punch that
decked all welterweights, our Kid stumbles through the clinics
of New York in worker's boots and his eye bulges from the ex-
cesses of the Revolution. They degraded the Kid and the Revolution and they sent him home with a red, white, and blue eye
patch. That's how they treated Kid Gavilan, and they'll do the
same to Achilles Alvarado."

"Well, goddamn," Zloto said, "I've had enough talk. I want
to see Alvarado; whether he wants to do it is up to him."

"That," Castro said, "is typical bourgeois thinking. You would
alienate the man from his fellows, let him think that his decision
is personal and lonely, that it represents only the whims of an
Alvarado and does not speak for the larger aspirations of all

Cubans, and all exploited peoples. The wants of an Alvarado are the wants of the people. He is not a Richard Nixon to hide out in Camp David surrounded by bodyguards while generals all over the world are ready to press the buttons of annihilation."

"No more bullshit, I want to see Alvarado."

Estelle said, "He is in Oriente Province on maneuvers with the army. He will be gone for . . . for how long, Fidel?"

"Achilles Alvadaro's unit is scheduled for six months in Oriente. I could bring him back to see you, Zloto, but we don't operate that way. A man's duty to his country comes before all else."

"Then I'm going up to see him and deliver the commissioner's letter. I don't trust anybody else around here to do it for me."

"We'll all go," Fidel said. "In Cuba Libre, no man goes it alone."

II
On Maneuvers in Oriente Province

The Ninth Infantry Unit of the Cuban Army is on spring maneuvers. Oriente is lush and hilly. There are villages every few miles in which happy farmers drink dark beer brewed with local hops. The Ninth Army bivouacs all over the province and assembles each morning at six a.m. to the sound of the bugle. The soldiers eat a leisurely breakfast and plan the next day's march. By two p.m., they are set up somewhere and ready for an afternoon of recreation. Colonel Alvarado is the only member of the Ninth Infantry with major-league experience, but there are a few older men who have played professional baseball in the minor leagues. Because there is no adequate protective equipment, army regulations prohibit hardball, but the Ninth Infantry plays fast-pitch softball, which is almost as grueling.

When Fidel, Zloto, and Estelle drive up to the Ninth Army's makeshift diamond, it is the seventh inning of a four–four game between the Reds and Whites. A former pitcher from Iowa City in the Three I League is on the mound for the Reds. Colonel

Alvarado, without face guard or chest protector, is the umpire behind the plate. His head, as in the old days, seems extremely vulnerable as it bobs behind the waving bat just inches from the arc of a powerful swing. He counts on luck and fast reflexes to save him from foul tips that could crush his Adam's apple.

When the jeep pulls up, Reds and Whites come to immediate attention, then raise their caps in an "Olé" for Fidel.

"These are liberated men, Zloto. The army does not own their lives. When their duties are completed they can do as they wish. We have no bedchecks, no passes, nobody is AWOL. If a man has a reason to leave, he tells his officer and he leaves. With us, it is an honor to be a soldier."

When Zloto spots Alvarado behind the plate he runs toward him and hugs his old friend. He rubs Alvarado's woolly black head with his oversize hands. Estelle is next to embrace her husband, a short businesslike kiss, and then Fidel embraces the umpire as enthusiastically as Zloto did. An army photographer catches the look of the umpire surprised by embraces from an old friend, a wife, and a Prime Minister in the seventh inning of a close game.

"Men of the Revolution." Fidel has advanced to the pitcher's mound, the highest ground. The congregated Reds and Whites gather around the makeshift infield. "Men of the Revolution, we are gathered here to test the resolve of your umpire, Colonel Alvarado. The Revolution is tested in many ways. This time it is the usual thing, the capitalist lure of money. Yet it is no simple issue. It is money that rightfully belongs to Colonel Alvarado, but they would degrade him by forcing him to claim it. To come there so that the capitalist press can say, 'Look what the Revolution has done to one of the stars of the fifties. Look at his stooped, arthritic back, his gnarled hands, from years in the cane fields.' They never cared about his inadequate English when they used him, but now they will laugh at his accent and his paltry vocabulary. When they ask him about Cuba, he will stumble and they will deride us all with the smiles of their golden teeth.

"The commissioner of baseball has sent us this behemoth, the Polish-American veteran of eleven campaigns in the American

League, Victor Zloto, who some of you may remember as Rookie of the Year in 1945. This Zloto is not an evil man, he is only a capitalist tool. They use his friendship for the colonel as a bait. Zloto speaks for free enterprise. He has two cars, a boat, and his own home. His province is represented by their hero of the right, Barry Goldwater, who wanted to bomb Hanoi to pieces. Zloto wants the colonel to come back, to go through the necessary charade to claim his rightful pension, and then return to us if he wishes. Mrs. Alvarado shares this view. I say no Cuban man should become a pawn for even one hour."

"What does the colonel say?" someone yells from the infield. "Does the colonel want to go back?"

The umpire is standing behind Castro. He is holding his wife's hand while Zloto's long arm encircles both of them. Castro turns to his colonel. "What do you say, Achilles Alvarado?"

Zloto says, "It's twelve grand a year, Archie, and all you have to do is show up just once. If you want to stay, you can. I know you don't like being a two-bit umpire and colonel down here. I know you don't give a shit about revolutions and things like that."

Castro says, "The colonel is thinking about his long career with the Chisox, Bosox, Tribe, and Birds. He is thinking about his four fractured skulls. He justifiably wants that pension. And I, his Prime Minister and his friend, I want him to have that pension, too. Believe me, soldiers, I want this long-suffering victim of exploitation to recover a small part of what they owe to him and to all victims of racism and oppression."

Colonel Alvarado grips tightly his wife's small hand. He looks down and kicks up clouds of dust with his army boots. He is silent. Zloto says, "It's not fair to do this, Castro. You damn well know it. You get him up here in front of the army and make a speech so it will look like he's a traitor if he puts in his pension claim. You staged all this because you are afraid that in a fair choice Archie would listen to reason just like Estelle did. You can bet that I'm going to tell the commissioner how you put Archie on the spot out here. I'm going to tell him that Archie is a softball umpire. This is worse than Joe Louis being a wrestling referee."

"Think fast, Yankee," one of the ballplayers yells as he lobs a softball at Zloto's perspiring face. The big first baseman's hand closes over the ball as if it were a large mushroom. He tosses it to Castro. "I wish we could play it out, Fidel, just you and I, like a world series or a one-on-one basketball game. I wish all political stuff could work out like baseball, with everybody where they belong at the end of the season and only one champion of the world."

"Of course, you would like that, Zloto, so long as you Yankee capitalists were the champions."

"The best team would win. If you have the material and the management, you win; it's that simple."

"Not as simple as you are, Zloto. But why should we stand here and argue political philosophy? We are interrupting a game, no? You have accused Fidel of not giving Alvarado a fair opportunity. I will do this with you, Zloto, if Achilles agrees, I will do this. Fidel will pitch to you. If you get a clean hit, you can take Alvarado back on the first plane. If not, Alvarado stays. It will be more than fair. This gives you a great advantage. A former big leaguer against an out-of-shape Prime Minister. My best pitch should be cake for you. You can go back and tell the commissioner that you got a hit off Castro. Barry Goldwater will kiss your fingertips for that."

Zloto smiles. "You're on, Castro, if it's okay with Archie and Estelle." Colonel Alvarado still eyes the soft dirt; he shrugs his shoulders. Castro says, "Do you think this is a just experience for you, Achilles Alvarado? This is like a medieval tournament, with you as the prize. This smacks of capitalism. But this once, Fidel will do it if you agree that your fate shall be so decided."

"What's all this about fate and justice," Estelle says. She takes the ball from Castro. "Archie had eleven brothers and sisters and hardly a good meal until he came up to the Chisox. He cracked his wrist in an all-star game and that cost him maybe four or five years in the big leagues because the bones didn't heal right. It's a mean, impersonal world with everything always up for grabs. Alvarado knows it, and he accepts it. He is a religious man." She throws the ball to her Prime Minister. "Get it over with."

The teams take their places, with Castro replacing the Three I League pitcher. Zloto removes his jacket, shirt, and necktie. He is six five and weighs over 250. His chest hairs are gray, but he swings three bats smoothly in a windmill motion as he loosens his muscles. Castro warms up with the catcher. The Prime Minister has a surprisingly good motion, more sidearm than underhand. The ball comes in and sinks to a right-handed batter like Zloto. Colonel Alvarado takes his place behind home plate, which is a large army canteen.

"Achilles Alvarado," says Castro, "you wish to be the umpire in this contest?"

"Why not?" Zloto says. "It's his pension, let him call the balls and strikes. If it's a walk or an error, we'll take it over. Otherwise, a hit I win, an out you win."

"Play ball!" the umpire says. Castro winds up twice, and his first pitch is so far outside that the catcher diving across the plate cannot even lay his glove on the ball. Fidel stamps his foot.

"Ball one," says the umpire.

The infield is alive with chatter: "The old dark one, Fidel," they are yelling. "Relax, pitcher, this ox is an easy out, he can't see your stuff, there's eight of us behind you, Fidel, let him hit."

Zloto grins at the Prime Minister. "Put it down the middle, Mr. Pink, I dare you."

Fidel winds and delivers. Zloto's big hands swing the bat so fast that the catcher doesn't have a chance to blink. He has connected and the ball soars a hundred feet over the head of the left fielder who watches with astonishment the descending arc of the power-driven ball.

"Foul ball," says the umpire, eyeing the stretched clothesline which ended far short of where Zloto's fly ball dropped.

The power hitter grins again. "When I straighten one out, Castro, I'm gonna hit it clear out of Cuba. I never played in a little country before."

Castro removes his green army cap and runs his stubby fingers through his hair. He turns his back to the batter and looks toward his outfield. With a tired motion he orders his center fielder to move toward left center, then he signals all three outfielders to move deeper. Estelle Alvarado stands in foul territory down the first-base line, almost in the spot of her complimentary box seat at the Chisox home games.

Zloto is measuring the outside corner of the canteen with a calm, deliberate swing. He does not take his eyes off the pitcher. Castro winds and delivers another wild one, high and inside. Zloto leans away but the ball nicks his bat and dribbles into foul territory, where Estelle picks it up and throws it back to Castro.

"One ball, two strikes," says the umpire.

"Lucky again, Castro," the batter calls out, "but it only takes one, that's all I need from you."

The Prime Minister and the aging Rookie of the Year eye one another across the sixty feet from mound to plate. Castro rubs the imagined gloss from the ball and pulls at his army socks. With the tip of a thin Cuban softball bat, Zloto knocks the dirt from the soles of his Florsheim shoes. The infielders have grown silent. Castro looks again at his outfield and behind it at the green and gentle hills of Oriente Province. He winds and delivers a low, fast ball.

"Strike three," says the umpire. Zloto keeps his bat cocked. Estelle Alvarado rushes to her husband. She is crying hysterically. Fidel runs in at top speed to embrace both Alvarados at home plate. Zloto drops the bat. "It was a fair call, Archie," he says to the umpire. "I got caught looking."

"Like Uncle Sam," Castro says as the soldiers stream in yelling, "Fidel, Fidel, the strike-out artist." Castro waves his arms for silence.

"Not Fidel, men, but Achilles Alvarado, a hero of the Cuban people. A light for the Third World."

"Third World for Alvarado. Third strike for Zloto," an infielder shouts as the Ninth Army raises Fidel, Achilles, and Estelle to their shoulders in a joyful march down the first-base line. The Prime Minister, the umpire, and the lady gleam in the sun like captured weapons.

Zloto has put on his shirt and tie. He looks now like a businessman, tired after a long day at a convention. Fidel is jubilant among his men. The umpire tips his cap to the army and calms his wife, still tearful atop the bobbing shoulders of the Cuban Ninth.

"Alvarado," Estelle says, "you honest ump, you Latin patriot, you veteran of many a clutch situation. Are you happy, you fractured skull?"

"Actually," Alvarado whispers in her ear, "the pitch was a little inside. But what the hell, it's only a game."

Gas Stations

Chances are you've been here too. World's largest, eighty-three pumps, forty-one urinals, advertised on road signs as far east as Iowa. Oasis, Wyoming, U.S. 40, hard to miss as you whiz on by. Even Jack Kerouac on an overnight cross-country spin used to stop here for soft ice cream. In the golden days they had their own tables, all those fifties beats, way in the back by the truckers' shower room. They lumbered in with the long haulers, left their motors running just like the diesel men, wore leather too and drank half cups of coffee. The truckers said "shit" more. Bus-boys, in retrospect, could tell them apart by the poems on the napkins.

The counter is fifteen yards long and there must be two hundred tables. The waitresses wear roller skates except when carrying expensive meals. Everyone chews gum. The girls are all named Ellie. At their waists, just above the apron, they make change like busdrivers out of metal slots. Quarters fly onto tables, dimes trickle down their legs.

I order hashbrowns and eggs, whole-wheat toast, and coffee. My Chevy is being gassed out front, pump number forty-eight. The place mat tells the incredible story of the man who made all this possible. He dreamed a dream fifty years ago on a cold hillside. He was a Wyoming shepherd boy nuzzled against members of his flock in the biting wind. He dreamed that all his bleating herds became Cashmere goats at five times the price, that Wyoming shriveled up and dove into Texas. He awoke with frostbitten ears, fingers iced into the wool he clutched.

While that man awaited the slow-rising sun to warm his limbs and awaken his herds, he vowed a vow.

"This won't be a barren wasteland," he vowed; "men will know that here I froze one night so that after this men shall freeze here no more." He slapped his herd with a long crook. His collies awoke as if it were spring and stretched on their forepaws. The man spit into the icy wind. He named the spot Oasis.

I look up from this saga on the place mat to recall, in the midst of travel, the tiny oasis of my youth, Ted Johnson's Standard. On our own block flew the Texaco star and the Mobil horse, but you couldn't pay us not to fill our Pontiac at Ted Johnson's Standard. He was the magician of the fan belt. With an old rag and one tough weathered hand, he took on radiators foaming and in flame. Where other men displayed girlie calendars, Ted Johnson hung the green cross of safety.

Although he looked like Smokey the Bear, it was engine neglect and rowdy driving that he cautioned against. Whenever a kid short-cut onto Bridge Street across his pumps, Old Ted raised the finger of warning. "Stay to the right, Sonny," he would yell, shaking his gray head over the lapse in safety. He had spotless pumps, his rest rooms glowed in the dark, he bleached the windshield sponges, but it was safety that drew us all to Ted. He wouldn't take your money until he had checked your spare. And it must have worked. He never lost a regular customer to a traffic fatality. He kept the number of deathless days posted above his cash register. At night, after he counted his receipts, Ted read the obituaries and added another safety day. I remember at least 7300. Twenty years of Ted's customers rolling down the road with their spare tires at the ready. They didn't need their suction-cup saints, Ted passed out his own stick-on mottos for the dashboard.

> Don't switch lanes
> Always signal first
> Use the rear view mirror

Yes, Ted Johnson's Standard, here in the middle of the world's biggest rest area, I long for you. They don't clean my windshield and my hood is tinkered with less than a fat girl's skirt. At night, Ted, they won't even make change and in the best of times you have to beg for the rest-room key.

You treated our cars, Ted, like princes from afar. The way Abraham must have washed the feet of angels, so you sponged windshields fore and aft. And those glass-headed pumps of yours looked like the Statue of Liberty lowering her torch to us, cozying up to our rear end.

My waitress rolls up. Her name is Ellie. "We're out of eggs," she says, "how about oatmeal? Twice the protein and none of that troublesome cholesterol. A man your age can't be too careful.

"I'm only thirty," I tell her.

"Not so young. In Korea, in the middle of veins, they found cholesterol at nineteen. The oatmeal's on special today. Think about it." I think about oatmeal while I continue the place-mat saga of Oasis, Wyoming. In 1930 there wasn't a road within a hundred miles. The shepherd boy was twenty-eight then and rode the freight to Grand Forks, South Dakota. With his stick and his collie and his dream, he rode east and almost succumbed, once in Kansas City and again in Chicago, to a fortune in the stockyards. By 1940 he had made a million in suet and owned a mansion on Lake Shore Drive. Big stock men from all over came by to sample his roast beef and pork chops and talk business. Swift and Armour sent him Christmas gifts. The dog was his only memento of Wyoming.

Still, the millionaire was restless. His vow came back to trouble him. The autumn of 1941 was the worst freeze Chicago ever knew. By October the leaves in all their splendor froze upon the limbs. Thanksgiving was twenty-two below zero, the average for November. People coughed chilled blood into the streets. The stockyards closed. On December 7 the Japanese attacked Pearl Harbor and the millionaire suet man knew who the Jonah was. "I hustled ass back to Wyoming," he said, "before the enemy could make it his own."

First he leveled the land and built towers of fluorescent lamps. There was still no road within fifty miles, but now the man thought of nothing but his vow. "The road will come," he said, and he invested his million in a pinball arcade, a small wax museum, and the earliest version of the restaurant. The gas pumps were an afterthought.

Ellie brings me oatmeal.

"No charge if you don't like it," she says. "They've got twenty pounds of it in the kitchen. It'll be lumpy by noon anyway." She looks over my shoulder while I taste. Her long hair touches the milk in the spoon, the steam rises to both our nostrils.

"It's good," I say.

"It has to be," Ellie answers; "the big boss eats it himself." She nods toward a bald man about twelve tables east of me. He wears a baggy thin-lapeled suit and is daydreaming through his smoky windows. When I finish breakfast I walk over to shake the hand of the man whose history has filled my place mat. He attempts to smile for me but can't quite do it.

"Troubles," I ask, "when you have eighty-three pumps and are a place-mat legend?" He collapses over the table. He buries his head in his hands.

"Personal problems?" I ask. "Health? marital? emotional?"

He picks up his head. "Psychiatrist?" he inquires.

"Only a traveler," I respond, "heading west." He sits up and looks around to make sure that nobody is listening to us. He pulls me close to his shrunken lips. "Arabs," he moans into my ear. "When they couldn't buy the Alamo they started putting the pressure on Oasis. They want Coney Island too and Disneyland. Our government is worrying about U.S. Steel and Armour beef, they don't know the desires of desert folk. I do. My people come from Lebanon, also a land of milk and honey."

To cheer the man I tell him about Ted Johnson's Standard, the example that has strengthened me through breakfast. "A white tile building," I tell him, "round as a mosque. Inside, it was like a solarium. Cut flowers bloomed from the carcasses of dried-out batteries. The Lions Club glass and the March of Dimes cup twinkled in their fullness. Only one grade of motor oil there, the very best, and six-ply treads, mufflers with welded reinforcements, belts and hoses of the finest Indian rubber..."

"Enough," says the Oasis man, "you're just a piss-call romantic mooning over the good old days of Rockefeller. Wake up. Ted's Standard belongs to OPEC now. It flies the sign of the Crescent. Turbaned attendants laugh at the idea of a comfort station. They mix foreign coinage in your change."

"What about your help?" I motion toward my Chevy, where a swarthy man peeks beneath the hood. He wipes the oil stick clean with his lips and spits into the radiator.

"Just Mormons in make-up," the Oasis man says. "You can't find a real Arab out here, but I do my best. I want to get the country ready for what's coming. I give out free headdresses all through the holy month of Ramadan. For a nickel I'll sell you an "Allah Lives" bumper sticker. We closed down on the day Faisal was assassinated. You can't buck the future."

"And what about the Ted Johnsons," I ask, "the men in uniform who made our stations great?"

"Underground," he says, "with the hat blockers and egg candlers, praying for the resurrection of the downtown."

"I don't believe it's so bleak," I say.

"Bleak for you and me," the Oasis man answers, "not so bleak along the Nile and the Euphrates. Every thousand years or so Mesopotamia gets a shot in the arm. It's just history. You can't buck it. You go along."

"I don't see it that way, Mr. Big, no sir, I don't."

Ellie rolls up with another ladle of oatmeal for the boss. "Beware," he says, "watch out for price fixing in radial tires and don't believe what the company tells you about STP." He rouses himself for a moment from his melancholy. "We serve three thousand meals a day here. Where are you headed, California?"

"Righto," I say, not even surprised that he has guessed it.

"Your own station or a dealer owned?"

"Franchise direct from J. Paul Getty, option to buy in five years." The Oasis man can tell that I'm proud of myself.

"Dummy," he says, "in five years you'll be a slave in Tunis." Ellie pulls up a chair and joins us.

"No," I say, "in five years I'll be like Ted Johnson. I'll be fixing flats and tuning engines in the happy hills outside San

Francisco. I'll have an '81 Chevy, loaded, and watch the Golden Gate Bridge hanging in the fog."

"More oatmeal for you two?" Ellie asks. "It'll all be lumps by noon." Her perfect legs in their black hose roll toward the kitchen. Sparks fly from her wheels.

"Young man," he tells me, looking away now through the window at what is visible from this angle of his eighty-three pumps, "take it from the King of Octane, there's not a fart's chance for you out there. Go back to school. Learn dentistry. The Third World will need attention to its teeth."

Ellie is back with oatmeal and hot coffee. She sits with us, makes a thin bridge out of her fingers, rests her chin on it as she stares at my oatmeal.

"You've had your day, Mr. Oasis," I tell him. "If the place mat is to be trusted, you've been hot and cold, rich and poor. Now you can sit at your window and watch the cash roll in. Ted Johnson never looked up except when he had a car on the rack. He called his place a service station. Your name was your credit over there."

The millionaire's mouth finally makes it into a huge smile. "How many pumps will you have?" he asks.

"Three," I tell him loudly. "One each, regular, premium, and no lead and no locks on the rest room." He breaks into giggles. People at other tables are looking but I don't care.

"That's right," I continue, "and rubber machines and ten-cent cokes if I can get them." He is almost rolling in the aisle now. Tears of happiness leak from the corners of his eyes. "Firecrackers and recaps, "I continue, "wheels balanced by hand, and even mufflers and pipes."

"Stop," he yelps amid his giggles. "I can't take any more." But I want to go on. "I'll lend out tools too and give a dollar's worth to anyone who's broke."

Ellie looks into my heart. "Take me with you," she says. "I'll check crankcase oil and clean windshields. I don't want to be a harem girl." Her look is as grim as mine. We leave him howling at the table. I pay my bill and buy her a pair of magnetic dogs. Beside my Chevy, Ellie removes her roller skates. Her black hose hooked around my antenna rise in the wind. Through the rear-view mirror I see in pursuit the disguised Mormons. Awkwardly they mount their camels and raise curved swords to the east. My electric starter drowns their desert shrieks. Three hundred and forty cubic inches rumble. I buckle up, Ellie moves close. Careful on the curves, amid kisses and hopes I give her the gas.

My
Real Estate

I

I have always believed in property. Though a tenant now, I have prospects. In fact, Joanne Williams, my realtor, thinks I have the greatest prospects in the world. She has always dropped in on me now and then, but these days she comes up almost every time she leaves her seat for popcorn or a coke. She brings her refreshment with her and she refreshes me. She has done so right from the start, ever since I first realized that I really wanted to own my own home.

She picked me up outside my apartment house. She gave me her card. We shook hands. She looked me over.

"You want a bungalow," she said, "two bedrooms, one and a half baths, central air, hardwood floors. You don't need the headache of a lawn."

In her big Oldsmobile we cruised the expressways. Short skirts were the style then. Joanne drove in bursts of speed. She was learning conversational Spanish from a Berlitz eight-track recording that played as we headed toward the fringes of the inner city, where she said there were "buys."

"*Haga me usted el favor de . . .*" said the tape.

"There are a lot of Spanish speakers entering the market," said Joanne. A small card on her dashboard, the type that usually says "Clergy," proclaimed, *Se Habla Espanol*. "Once you show someone a house," she said, "it's a moral obligation. You take them in your car, buy them lunch, introduce them to some homes in their price range. It's as if you've been naked together." She had long thin legs, all shin until they disappeared only a few inches below where her panty hose turned darker. When the tape ended, she asked if I was a wounded veteran and then if I had ever been in the army at all. She was sorry.

"With a VA loan you could float into a house. Conventional will be tougher. Still, you've got thirty years to cushion one or two percent." She shrugged her small shoulders, asked me about how much I earned.

I declined to say. Her skirt edged higher. I never knew what a VA loan meant. When I saw the VA signs around the housing developments, I thought that the whole thing was exclusively for veterans, that there were lots of crutches and wheelchair ramps and VFW halls in there. She laughed when I told her this.

"There is a lot to know in real estate." She was twenty-eight, she said, and divorced from a man who had liked furnished apartments. My efficiency in the beams is also furnished, but with great luxury. Simmons' Hide-A-Bed, chrome-and-glass coffee table, Baker easy chair, Drexel maple bed and dresser. There is a hunting tapestry on my living-room wall. My bathroom fixtures are gold leaf and the tub has a tiny whirlpool. When she wants nothing else, Joanne sometimes comes up just to soak her toes in the hot bubbles.

When she was the salesperson and I the client, she told me I was her first bachelor. "I know your type," she said. "When I went to singles' bars, you were all I ever met. You think apartments are where you'll meet people, you believe the managers who show you game rooms and swimming pools. Listen to how people talk. In apartments they don't have 'neighbors'; they say, 'He lives in my complex.' If you want to meet people, you buy a house."

Joanne refused to believe that I wanted a house for reasons other than neighbors and schools. "So what if you have no wife and children," she said, "why not be near kids that are well educated, less likely to soap your windows on Halloween and put sugar in your gas tank."

I told her the simple truth. "I want a house because my people have owned land and houses in Texas for four generations. We lived here with the Mexicans and the Indians. I'm the first Spenser who hasn't owned a tiny piece of Texas."

"You still can live with Mexicans and Indians," she told me, "in the Fifth Ward. But if you go there, you'll go without me."

She drove extravagantly and used no seat belts. I slid toward her on all the turns. She used the horn but not while listening to the tape. "In the suburbs," Joanne said, "I can put you into a two bedroom plus den and patio for eighteen five. I can get you all electric kitchens and even sprinkler systems for a lot less than you'll pay for an old frame bungalow close in." But no matter what she said, she couldn't convince me to look at Sharpstown and Green Acres and Cascade Shores. They sounded like Hong Kong and Katmandu. I grew up in Houston and never knew about these far-away places until I started noticing some of the addresses printed on the checks we took in at the store. Sometimes it was a long distance call to trace down a local bad check.

"My great-grandfather fought at the Alamo," I told her. "He was one of those who left when Santa Anna gave them a last chance. My grandad owned a farm near where the Astrodome is now." This was the first time the Dome entered our conversation. Joanne was unimpressed and it didn't seem very important to me either. The Dome was just another big building, the colonel who owned it, just another big businessman, and my grandad just another old memory, dead fifteen years.

In my case she was wrong about the suburbs, but Joanne did have an instinct for a client's needs. She was flexible. The one thing she could not do was pretend to like a house. If she didn't like the place, she got out fast, sometimes without leaving her card. She held her nose all the way to the car and refused to answer questions about the place. "Go back without me," she said, "go alone or take a lawyer or an interior decorator." Even when she liked a house, she made the home owners open their drapes. "I want to see everything in the bright light," she said. She came into a house like an actress to center stage. Buyers and sellers moved close to the walls. She sized places up as she walked through in long strides. She noticed inaccuracies in thermostats and recommended plasterers and electricians as she passed needed repairs. Whenever there was a child, she chased him down to pat his head. On our first day we spent three hours together. At four thirty, she told me there was a Mexican couple, thus the tape. At seven there was an Open House in Sharpstown. I should call her in the morning.

The next day, Sunday, she was at my door at eight a.m. She had a tennis dress so white that it literally blinded me as the sun reflected from it into my dark apartment.

"Sorry to wake you," she said, "but I was in the neighborhood and I need to use a phone, please." While I showered she made what seemed like dozens of calls. She had played tennis from six to eight. "Sunday is my big day. I have three listings in Montrose and one in Bel Air. With good weather we'll close something today." She joined me for what was her second breakfast. I knew that as she ate she was itemizing my establishment and judging my taste. She was doing even more than I thought. We finished breakfast at eight forty-five. "I don't have to be in Bel Air until ten fifteen," she said, and took off her tennis dress.

Joanne's style was intact, flawless, efficient. She was done in time to have a quick shower herself and give me a brief run-down on mortgage rates.

Later in the week, as she led me from house to house, I learned more personal information, facts from the life of Joanne Williams. She rattled them off as briskly as the square footage of a room. Born in Chicago, moved to Houston at fourteen, married high-school sweetheart; at twenty-five, childless, living in a furnished apartment where Chuck still resided only a few complexes east of me; left Chuck and job as legal secretary; became cocktail waitress. There amid "tips that would make your head swim," she met Vince, her sales manager. "What the hell," Vince asked her, "is a girl with your personality doing as a waitress? You should be out on the street." He opened his Multiple Listings book and started to show her some pictures. "There's a five-bedroom rancher that can bring you a four-thousand-dollar commission." Vince told her to think of herself as an obstetrician.

A house on the market was like a pregnant woman. She had to go, she would burst if nobody helped. You wanted to make it fast, painless, smooth.

She worked days for Vince, nights as a waitress. "At the end of the month I sold that five-bedroom rancher that Vince had randomly picked out of the book." "It was no accident," he said, "it was your career. I showed you the picture of it." She sold close to a million dollars in each of her first two years. This year she wanted to go over.

"The kind of house you want is chickenfeed," she told me, "but I've got the time for it. And who knows, you might one day have a rich friend who'll use me to buy a mansion in Green Meadows."

Because I was in the eighteen-to-twenty-two-thousand range with conventional mortgage, mediocre credit, and less than ten percent down, Joanne could not give me her best hours. I drew dinner times and late nights usually, but this made it convenient for us to eat and occasionally sleep together. She did not have to mix business and pleasure, any more than she had to hurry. Speed and pleasure and business all combined in her like the price and sales tax. The only noise she made was a small grinding of the teeth like a nervous signature on a deed. We rarely kissed and used only the most explicit embraces.

And Joanne did not pressure me to buy a house. As I wavered and mused upon closing costs and repair bills and termites and cockroaches, she just paid less and less attention to me. Finally, in spite of mutual fondness, we never saw each other at all. I kept up with her though by her signs around the city. She married Vince, but because his Italian name was so long they both used hers. Williams and Williams signs, bright orange with a green border sprang up throughout various better neighborhoods. Whenever I saw the sign, I knew that there Joanne had once opened drapes and frightened owners. She and Vince made a good team. He ran the office and took care of all the paperwork. This left her free to sell. Judging by the frequency of her signs, I guessed she now sold many millions in a year and had forgotten me as a truly bad investment of her time.

I underestimated her loyalty and her memory. Months after

our last encounter I met her in the express lane at Krogers. It was around supper time and she was buying three Hershey bars.

"With all the money you must earn now," I asked, "can't you take time out for a regular dinner?"

"Sweetheart," Joanne told me, "you never did understand real estate." She bought me a Hershey bar too. I left my less-than-purchases in the cart and followed her to a long white Cadillac. "Deductible," she said, "might as well." She made a U-turn and parked across the street among a group of vans belonging to plumbers who had gone home for the evening. She checked the clock on the panel. "I should be in River Oaks in thirty minutes to show five bedrooms, but they'll wait a few minutes if they have to."

They didn't have to. In the back seat of the Cadillac Joanne was her old self. I looked up and saw wrenches and plungers hanging from the ceilings of the plumbers vans. "I haven't forgotten you, Jack," she said. "Every time I see a two bedroom one bath in the medical-center area I mean to give you a call."

"Congratulations," I said, "on your marriage [I had read about it in the financial pages, they took out a quarter-page ad] and your own business."

"Yes," she said, "it's wonderful. If interest stays down we might even go into our own development."

II

When I next saw her, it was at my own apartment complex. I was on the balcony looking out at the tennis courts below me. Joanne saw me, halted her doubles match, and invited me to bring them all some cokes after the set.

Vince was as tall as Joanne but so thickset that she seemed to tower above him. He played the net and she took the long ones that he couldn't reach. She wore a tennis dress exactly like the one I remembered. Joanne introduced me to my landlords, Ben and Vera Bloom.

"'I'm glad to have a tenant like you," Ben Bloom said. "You

know the kind of people that usually rent these, twenty-two year olds that like to drink beer and screw and write on the walls. They never dump their garbage, but every time they see a roach they run to call the manager. You can't satisfy people like them. No matter what you do they move out. They break leases. Who's going to take a traveling salesman to court?"

Vince treated me like an old friend, claimed that he recognized my name as a former client of their old company. When he and Joanne went into the business for themselves, most of the old company came along with them. "We closed the deal for the land you're standing on," Vince said, "so you might say we did a little bit to help you find a place." He seemed to feel guilty that their company had not matched me with a house. "It's his own fault," Joanne said, "he had chances; by the time he decides someone else has put in a bid."

"Oh, one of those," Vince said. Still he invited me to join them that night at the ball game. The Astros were playing the Cubs. "I've never been to the Dome," I admitted.

"It's a separate world," Ben Bloom said. He wiped the perspiration from his eyes and took off his tennis glove. "People like me put up these developments and tract houses and zoned subdivisions, but not the Colonel. The Colonel left us to fuck around with the small stuff. He went for the pie in the sky."

"And he made it," Vera said; "he put us on the map more than the moon did. Nobody even remembers the moon any more, but just mention Houston at a convention and they all ask about the Dome."

They were going to a party celebrating the fifth anniversary of the stadium. Joanne asked me to meet them at the Colonel's penthouse.

That night, watched by ushers and security guards, I entered the penthouse in the beams. I felt underdressed in my corduroy trousers and sports shirt. Joanne, I noticed, was wearing a black dress with a cut-out back, but Vince was as casually dressed as I. They made me feel very comfortable in the Colonel's living room. The Blooms were there and many other couples. The tuxedoed ushers carried trays full of martinis and Tom Collinses.

"It's a nickel-beer night in the grandstand," Vince said. "No matter how much you drink you won't be able to keep up with the slobs down there. You couldn't get me to nickel-beer night. They piss down all the corridors leading to the men's rooms."

Joanne took me by the elbow and introduced me to some guests. She was relaxed and elegant. I had never seen her in company before, only in business and in bed. She was not even wearing a watch.

"What can I do," she told me when I asked, "I'm here for the evening just like the baseball players. When there's nothing to do, I play ball. That's something else you don't know about real estate."

If I could have looked out from this Dome toward the east, I would have seen my grandfather's former seventy-five acres only a city block away. There are gas stations and motels on the property now and the roller coaster of an amusement park. My grandfather died broke in the Christian Brothers Home for the Aged. He sold his land right before World War II to buy a liquor store. My dad ran the store.

While I was thinking what might have been if Grandad had held onto the land instead of going into the liquor business, the Colonel rolled in, a big gray-bearded man in an expensive-looking wheelchair. An Astros blanket lay across his knees. A nurse in white and an usher in her gown stood on each side of the chair. Ben Bloom proposed a toast. "To the head of the Dome," he said, "to the man who made it all possible." We clinked our glasses. The Colonel could neither drink nor hold the glass.

"A bad stroke," Joanne whispered to me, "during the first football season. He's never even felt the AstroTurf, poor man." She smiled and went over to pat the Colonel on the shoulder. He seemed to understand everything but could barely speak.

As the nurse wheeled him through the guests, it came my turn to meet the great man. The room seemed more crowded, Joanne was nowhere in sight.

"Jack Spenser, sir," I said, not really knowing how to explain my presence, "my grandfather once owned seventy-five acres on Old Spanish Trail. I'd like to buy myself a house in this area."

I could not be sure if he had even heard me. The nurse pushed with some effort his polished chair over the thick carpeting. The room was quite full now, of people with drinks and loud voices. Nobody was watching the TV or cared about the game itself hundreds of feet below.

"Lyndon Johnson used to stay in this suite," I heard someone say, "and get drunk on his ass for the whole weekend. He'd send the Secret Service out to the ranch so everyone would think he was there worrying about Vietnam. It would have taken a pretty shrewd assassin to look for him way up at the top of the Dome."

The splendor of the Astrodome was not the baseball I knew. My dad and I used to go to Texas league games at Haynes Stadium for Saturday-night doubleheaders. We packed a lunch and a lot of mosquito repellent and sat out in the bleachers for twenty-five cents each. My hero was a black first baseman named Eleazer Brown who never made it to the big leagues. He was six foot eight and for a while did play with the Globetrotters. When my dad closed the liquor store after the eighth robbery and his second bullet wound, the police brought him to a line-up to identify one of the hold-up men. It was a cinch. Dad knew the big torso of Eleazer Brown even when Eleazer was slouched over and in dark glasses. "It was a sad day for me," Dad said, "fingering that coon who could hit the ball five hundred feet. That's him, I told the cops, and you know, in spite of everything, I almost went up and asked that black bastard for his autograph." At least Brown hadn't shot at Dad; it was his friend who did that, an average-sized numbers runner from Dallas.

The roof of the Dome was so high, I had read, that you could put the Shamrock Hotel into it. I tried to imagine the biggest thing I could, the Goodyear blimp, dwarfed against the ceiling. As a store manager I was entitled to one ride a year in the blimp. When I first met Joanne, I had taken her as my guest. She pointed out landmarks to the children of other managers. When we landed, she ran toward her car. "It made me nervous," she said, "it reminded me of a mobile home."

"I've been looking for you," Joanne said. "The Colonel wants to see you. He never asks for anybody."

"Why does he want me?"

"Who knows," Joanne said, "but it's a great honor. Vince and Ben thought you went down to the game. Go ahead, he's in the other room with his nurse." I knocked at the door.

The Colonel and his nurse awaited me in a smaller sitting room. I was surprised that he smoked a pipe. The nurse held it for him between puffs. As I waited for the Colonel to begin, the nurse played with the pipe stem. With a small knife she shaved the dark tobacco and repacked the bowl. She caressed the stem. It took the Colonel a long time to say anything. He had to get his mouth in the right position. I could see how difficult it was for him. When he did begin, the words came out loud and uneven, like a child writing on a blackboard.

"Your grandpa," he got out, "was a dumbass son of a bitch." He puffed on the pipe and then the nurse repacked it. I waited for the second sentence.

"He could have had a piece of the world . . . wanted a liquor store instead." As the Colonel, between puffs and silences, got out his story I learned that he had bought most of the Dome land from Grandad and had offered my ancestor a part of what, at that time, was going to be a housing development. Just as I hesitated with Joanne over my would-be bungalow, so Gramps had hemmed and hawed with the Colonel and finally taken his money instead for the liquor-store enterprise.

"We grew up together on the Buffalo Bayou," the Colonel said. "He sold booze during prohibition and never forgot that he made easy money then. Before he kicked off, I told him about the Dome and he laughed in my face. Now," the Colonel went on even more slowly, "now the laugh is on me. I put the top on baseball. I made my own horizon. I shut out the sky. But I've got no arms and no legs and no sons and no daughters." He took a long, long pause and rejected the pipe. The noise from the party in the outer rooms surrounded our silence. It made the Colonel's slowness even more dramatic.

"I never liked Old Jack Spenser [I was named for Grandad], and I jewed him out of his land. Fifty bucks an acre was a steal even in those days. He had liquor on his mind all the time."

While the Colonel kept pausing, I tried to remember what I

actually had heard about the land on the Old Spanish Trail. I knew it had been Gramps' land, but when he went senile I was just a boy. All I remember is his crazy laugh in the Christian home. We used to have to bring him dolls when we came as if he were a baby. He died in '56, and Dad only made it two years beyond that. The liquor store was busted. Mom moved to Colorado with my sister.

"For a liquor store, he gave up this." With difficulty the Colonel made a neck gesture that suggested arms wide open. "I can't stand all these outsiders that keep coming down here. I'd like the Dome to be just for us Texans. That real-estate girl told me you wanted your own house. You're smarter than your grandad." Then the Colonel made me an offer. I thought about it overnight, asked Joanne's advice the next day. "I only think of single dwellings," she said, "the family is the unit I work with. Ask someone who knows big spaces." But without further advice I did it on my own. What was there to lose?

III

That was almost three years ago. Now, I don't work for Goodyear any more. I don't have to. The Colonel pays me two hundred a week plus room. He only leaves the Dome to go to the doctor's office in Plaza Del Oro across the street. I have my own apartment next to his and my only real job is getting up to turn the Colonel at three each morning so he won't get bedsores. The night watchman lets me in. The Colonel is asleep on his right side. He snores quietly into his beard. Since I'm pretty tired too, it's all a blur. I pull the special pad from beneath his hips and put it on the other side of him. I grab his arms as if they're ropes and give a good hard pull, then I go back to the other side of the bed and roll his hips over. He never wakes up.

Lately Joanne has been saying that I'll inherit the Dome someday because he's got no heirs. "He picked you because you're a Texan, because he knew your grandpa. He doesn't need other reasons. What else is he going to do with it?" When she tells me how rich I'm going to be, she snuggles up close and spends an extra few minutes. The high interest rates since '73 have really hurt her business and her marriage. She doesn't talk about it too much, but things are not working out between her and Vince. "He wants to go commercial," she says; "I can't work beyond the family. He wants to use leverage. He talks about a real-estate trust. I look at houses as walls and roofs. Vince calls them instruments and units." They have filed for divorce.

This year, for the first time, Joanne bought an Astros season ticket. Sometimes I go down to watch an inning or two, and when I come back, there she is in my whirlpool. She is as fast and smooth as ever. Interest rates and marriage have not changed her. She doesn't look around for Jack Spenser's perfect house any longer. "You'll own the Dome soon," she says; "you'll call all the shots."

I don't think the Colonel is likely to make me his heir but there is no doubt that it's possible. He calls for me every few weeks just to talk. He's getting weaker but he still likes to tell me what a dumbass Grandpa was. I agree and have taken over the nurse's job with the pipe. So far it's been no real problem. If the Colonel wants to call Grandad a dumbass all the time, that's his privilege.

In most ways my life is pretty much the same, but living in the Dome has killed my interest in baseball. When I do watch an inning or two, it's only to look at the scoreboard or the mix of colors in the crowd or to listen to the sound of the bat meeting the ball. What I like to do most is walk behind the grandstand and watch the people buying refreshments. There are one hundred twenty-six places in the Dome where you can buy beer. People line up at every one of them. There are eight restaurants and six of them have liquor licenses. While Astros and Dodgers and Cubs and Giants are running the bases and hitting the balls, the Colonel is making a fortune on beer and liquor. My Grandpa, I think, wasn't such a dumbass. He just had the wrong location.

Joanne has lots of plans for later. She wants to marry me. She says that we could keep the name of her business and use all the signs she has left over from her years with Vince.

"We won't need the money," I tell her, "we'll take a vacation around the world."

"No," she says, "first we'll evict the baseball team and the conventions. We can make a big profit on these auditorium seats. Then we'll put up modern bungalows, just the kind you wanted. They'll be close to downtown and have every convenience. There's room here for dozens. Even the outdoors will be air-conditioned. We'll put good private schools in the clubhouses and lease all the corridor space for shops and supermarkets. A few condominiums down the foul lines," she says, "and a hospital in center field. The scoreboard will be the world's biggest drive-in movie."

I go along with her. She gets more passionate when she talks this way, more involved with me. She's been saying these things for quite a while now and keeping track of the Colonel's health. He is so slow these days that he falls asleep between words. I don't think he can last much longer. Joanne gets very excited when she sees his pale face being wheeled past my door. "We'll move into his place," she says, "and use this as my office." I'm sad when I think of the Colonel becoming something like my Grandpa playing with dolls, but I didn't take Joanne too seriously until a few days ago when after some drinks and a whirlpool bath she put on a long hostess gown and went back to her box behind third base. I followed because I was suspicious of the gown. She walked right over the railing onto the field. She took the third-base umpire by the arm and led him to the mound. "Let's get some sunlight in here," she yelled to the top of the Dome, "let's see what it would be like with new tenants. It's a good neighborhood. There's a lots of shade and well-kept lawns, and the neighbors"—she looked at Walt Alston in the visitors' dugout—"the neighbors seem friendly and sincere." She left the umpire at the pitcher's mound and started taking her long strides toward the outfield.

"Rates can't go much higher," she told the Dodger infield, "but if they do you'll be extra glad you bought now. A house isn't like other investments. Stocks and bonds don't give you the direct benefits of housing. There is nothing else like it on God's earth. Yearly deductions, shelter, comfort, and all of it at capital-gains rates."

"Do you have children?" she asked the second baseman, who looked on in bewilderment. "If you do you'll appreciate the lack of traffic. You can send three-year-olds to the store without any worries." By center field her stride was almost a gallop. "Don't worry," she called to the Dodgers' black left fielder, "you'll be able to live here too. It will take a few years, but the whole world is changing."

A squadron of park policemen caught up with her on the way to the bullpen. They led her back to the third-base box, where I waited alongside the manager, who knew me and told the police to let her go in my custody. The policemen were gentle with her and the crowd cheered as she put those long smooth legs easily over the high railing. She threw kisses in all directions. The scoreboard spelled out "charge" and the organist played "Funny Girl." I led her up the ramp toward the escalator. "The place will sell, Jack. Everybody loves it. That AstroTurf will save a bundle on gardening too. We can do it, Jack, I know we can. When the Colonel leaves it to you, can we go ahead with it?"

She was all motion in my apartment. I could hardly restrain her from going into the Colonel's penthouse and strangling him with a pillow. "I'm only kidding about that," she said. "We're at the top now, we can wait."

As she ran the water for another whirlpool bath to relax her I thought of my great-grandfather saying good-bye to Davy Crockett and walking out of history, his son selling out to the Colonel, and my own dad bankrupt by liquor. Far below us someone was stealing a base. Next door the Colonel was struggling for a word. Cartoons blinked from the scoreboard. I took off my clothes. "It must run in the family," I said, thinking of Gramps laughing in the empty hallway of the Christian Brothers Home. I laughed out loud too. "If I get the Dome, do anything you want with it," I said. "Just save me room for the world's largest liquor store." In the midst of bubbles, I joined her. We sparkled like champagne.

Think of me as two hundred and sixty-three lines of broken light per second scattered through twenty-one years. Prick me and I short. In a sense, it explains everything, in a sense . . .

It does not. Television is television and murder is murder. The Senate subcommittee hearings on violence and TV reached no final conclusions, nor did the Eisenhower (Milton) committee or the Kerner commission. I'm sorry to sound so factual, so lawyer-ish, but we agreed to be honest with each other. Remember?

Okay, but my parents were married on *Bride and Groom* in 1952 just when TV started to explode, when the cities grew antennas like baseball gloves. I have the kinescope of Mom and Dad and Bud Collyer. A happy organ leads into Bud's solemn, "Kenneth Cook of Cleveland, Ohio, and Edith White of Elmira, New York . . ." You see a cameo close-up of Edith, then of Ken. They're locked arm in arm, but, you know, when I used to watch it as a kid I thought she was in New York and he was in Cleveland. I thought they only looked together the way Walter Cronkite and Eric Sevareid do no matter where they are. I thought that Edith and Ken only got together after that Ivory Soap commercial when Bud said, "And now the nation is wait-ing to hear a tale of love and heroism, another chapter in America's matrimonial pastime, *Bride and Groom.*" Bud was really something. He could wring a story out in fifteen minutes without getting maudlin like Jack Bailey. But Edith, she was a decade too early. In color and on something like *The Price Is*

Right she would have been a killer. A slip of the tongue. What I mean is she had a long horsy face, but zip, fire, a personality. It explains a part of me. *Bride and Groom* was not her vehicle. All she could do on that show was look solemn as if a fuck would do her in. She tapped her eyes with a white lace hanky while Bud ran down Dad's medals. He had "courage to spare," Bud said. That explains another part of me. Bud read a letter from General Ridgeway saying that Kenneth Cook was a credit to the U.S. Army. Ken Cook belched in Bud's face and that cagey pro said, "*Gesuntheit.*" I've run it back dozens of times. It's a genuine drunken, stinking belch from way down deep. It would have knocked you or me back into the camera, but Bud never blinked. That's a pro for you. Also a credit to the nation.

I'm willing to listen if you really think this is important to the case.

It is the case. No *Bride and Groom*, no me. My beginning and my end is television. It's too bad they abolished the death penalty. Now there's nothing theatrical in criminal law. A man's life is not at stake, only a certain kind of boredom. The defendant is hereby ordered bored to death in prison rather than in Elmira or Cincinnati. It's a shame I couldn't have done this in the good old days. I'd make them forget Caryl Chessman in a hurry. You lawyers have it made all right, you come out golden. Not even a ghost to haunt you when you blow one. Fifty bucks an hour and a clean conscience.

I earn nothing from your case, I am court appointed. You seem to forget that wealth is not one of your qualities. You're not Lee Harvey Oswald and I'm not Perry Mason. Let's go on.

I won't plead insanity.

You wouldn't have a chance, you planned too carefully. But with luck and a sympathetic jury you might come off with second degree or maybe even manslaughter.

My childhood should count for second degree. Manslaughter is a misnomer. I killed one of the seven deadly sins, the electric version of Horatio Alger. I have no guilt, no remorse. I felt worse when I stepped on ants in the second grade. As I was saying, their wedding film is the major memory of my childhood.

We had no black-box Kodaks, no snaps of me month by month, no marks along the wall to measure junior's growth. Suddenly, there I was fourteen with acne and hard-ons. The only thing I know about my father is the way he looked in that fifteen-minute segment of *Bride and Groom*. He wore his army uniform full of ribbons and medals. She said the producers told him to because that's what they wanted him to talk about, that he'd been a war hero. He also did not own a suit. She was already pregnant. If they'd known, probably the producers wouldn't have let her on the show. Things were very wholesome in those days. Bud Collyer said God Bless You at the end of the wedding. It wouldn't surprise me if every girl on *The Dating Game* takes the pill and I don't believe they send any chaperones on those pre-honeymoon trips either. Don't look so impatient counselor, I told you that television was the subject so I'm not just making sand castles. This is part of my defense. Because my mother was pregnant, I too am a member of the *Bride and Groom* cast. That fifteen-minute filmstrip and the Bell and Howell projector that brings it to life are my inheritance and my history. The ragtag Kroehler North Carolina sofa that I now use as porch furniture was one of the gifts to the newlyweds, so is the Sunbeam toaster popping to this day. Mother died in the wreck of a '54 DeSoto downpaymented with the three hundred in cash from the show.

If not for *Bride and Groom*, they would never have married. She was only two weeks pregnant and he had probably kicked in a few bellies with his pointed-toe Stetsons. He had been drunk since before the war ended. I don't think he ever knew exactly who she was and she only wanted the prizes. The producer made up a little history of how they met. She was working in a drugstore in Elmira and noticed his medals when he came in for a bottle of cough medicine. A nice twist, the girl noticing his chest. She was demure in a black cotton servant's outfit set off with a gingham apron. Miss Soda Fountain amid the pharmacists, coy as doctors, opening brown Latinate bottles in the back room. Her chipped and polished fingernails moved a damp rag across the counter where his heroic elbows were soon to rest. "Got any cough syrup?" he asks, not even coughing to seem authentic. Not a cringe, not a blink from either. Eyes meet. She clutches the rag like it's money in the wind. His Purple Heart tinkles like a nickel against the counter. She inhales. Awed by the spectacle of his chest, her own bosom grows toward his asymmetrical eyes. "What kindja want?" She points to expectorants, but his eye stays on her tit like it's a rifle sight and he's about to machine-gun the row of glasses and the angular mirrors making pieces out of them behind her. "Is it love at first sight?" asks Bud. "Yes," they coo on national television, holding sweaty palms, their cheeks be-rouged, the camera grinding out for their son this moment and no other. But in the drugstore it is different. She leans farther, her black outfit exhaling starch to his nostrils still soaked in the Orient. He has smelled war women, blood and dirt hopping on his cock like seals jumping for sardines. "G.I. fuckee wuckee." No sir. This American snatch comes down on him cool as the eucalyptus in his cough syrup, a cross between her tits. Jesus really did die here, drowned by the trickling sweat of hours on her feet peddling cokes to crew cuts who say "Gee whiz" and wait like saints for the next three-dimensional comic book.

"And that love at first sight brought this inspirational story to us. We thank you Ken and Edith for sharing it with America." First she shared herself in the basement of the drugstore at lunch hour, lounging over the cases of Budweiser empties. Even then he is almost too drunk to unhook his army belt, but she is gentle as Florence Nightingale. And there I come, a phoenix from the empties, while she claws his khaki shirt and bites in half a dis-tinguished-service medal. You should have settled for the cough syrup, Ken. For your ailment she offered only what you had rent too often with soft-nosed bullets. She told me none of it was true, but I believe it all; the story as told on *Bride and Groom* is my cosmogony. I would sooner give up Adam and Eve, Abra-ham, Noah. . . .

Please, let's get on to 1973. You could spend hours on 1952.

I will when I take the stand. You'll see. If you're in a hurry don't show up for the trial. It will be my Harvard and my Yale, my novel and my family. I am going to filibuster the legal sys-tem. They'll have to gag me like Bobby Seale. I want to be remembered as the most eloquent murderer in American history. Maybe they'll do a TV series based on my life. I could be a consultant and have a fat salary in prison. By the way, are you taping this? Good. Maybe we can just play the tape and I won't have to repeat it all in court. We can put the little Sony on the Bible, I'll preread the "I solemnly swear" part, then we can cut right to the soundtrack from *Bride and Groom*. "Do you, Edith White, take this man, Kenneth Cook? . . ." It would make all the connections without my having to explain again. With good editing the tape could even anticipate some questions from the state.

Please.

All right. We agree that no murder is simple, although the act is as easy as brushing your teeth. You've gone to law school— I've read *Crime and Punishment*. Neither of us probably believes most of what we've learned. I find zero similarity between myself and Raskolnikov. I am closer to those unknown anarchists who threw bombs at czars just like cheerleaders being flowered in confetti.

Please.

All right. I grew up doing two things at once. Watching television and whatever else was at hand. Usually homework or dishwashing. My high-school job was in the very drugstore where they met, changed only by the addition of a TV blaring all the time. Most recently I was a security man at National Department Store. My entire job was watching people move around the store, on a seven-inch closed-circuit screen. I could switch channels from say lingerie to sporting goods to the main door, but mostly they wanted me to keep my eyes on girls' sportswear and the record department.

A voyeur's dream that job was. I sat alone in an office created by combining three dressing rooms. The door was marked SECURITY—KEEP OUT. On my little screen were girls pulling dresses off the racks, standing in front of full-length mirrors gazing at what they might be with a few yards of new cotton or rayon. I didn't see them naked, of course, that would have been crude as well as illegal. I saw them in the mirror as they stood fully clothed, holding the new thing in front of them with the plastic hanger at their neck looking like a forked goiter. They had to decide which ones to try on. "Three dress limit in the dressing room," the sign said. They had to be careful, these little Cinderellas. Careful not to take their clothes off or squander a whole lunch hour on any old dress. I watched their eyes for the decision-making process. With the right camera angle I could always tell a thief. A customer loves that dress or record she is about to buy. She thinks of what her friends will say about her in the new hiphuggers. In a thief's eyes there is no lust. Even when she truly desires the object, she has only a job to do. The pleasure must come later when she is alone with her reward.

I think psychologists and other security men might disagree with that.

They would be wrong.

Please, let's get on with your account of that day.

I can't tell it any faster. Don't they teach legal etiquette. Just because I'm sane doesn't mean I have to expedite the case, does it? Anytime you want out, just say so Mr. Court Appointee. If they talk to me, I could probably get F. Lee or Percy Foreman or Melvin Belli . . . I don't know the names of any other lawyers.

Okay, I'm sorry for rushing you, you're my last interview this afternoon and I'm not hungry.

A pity. I was going to invite you to stay for dinner. The prison food is better than I'm accustomed to, living alone as I have for three years—make note of this for my defense—living alone for three years eating pork and beans, Dinty Moore stews, Chef Boyardee spaghetti. I use nothing uncanned. For some reason I am suspicious of both the frozen and the fresh. The fresh I suppose because it is all too easily and quickly subject to decay, the frozen because it is cold against my breast as I walk the three blocks from the supermarket.

The cans are heavier than frozen foods, aren't they?

A good point, counselor; obviously my major interest is in conserving heat.

Let's not get cute.

You started it—but again the point is made. I came to California for the heat, not to get Larry Love. I never even watched *Trade or Betrayed* my first few months here. I came for the year-round sun and it has cleared my skin.

When did you first see Larry Love?

I saw him in a drugstore in Beverly Hills.

And you recognized him?

I did.

Did you speak to him?

I tried. My hate was immediate and sincere. He was buying a hairbrush. The salesclerk fawned over him. I was eating an ice-cream cone, my uncanned luxury. He was tall and strong look-ing, much handsomer than he seemed on my fourteen-inch black-and-white Admiral. "Larry," I said to him.

"I haven't got time now, friend, watch the show and I'll think of you." He was gone to a waiting Cadillac illegally parked. He should have stayed for the end of my sentence, it was really his sentence. "Larry, I'm going to kill you." He missed the crucial part. Larry Love and Pontius Pilate left too soon for answers.

But why did you decide to kill him, why not other emcees, other stars?

Have you ever watched *Trade or Betrayed*?

Only in the last week, since I've taken your case. I can see that Larry must have been the show, it's not much without him.

Of course not, would Hell be the same without Satan?

Let's be legal, not theological. I would like a simple statement of why on April 7, 1973, you, in full view of millions, shot and killed Larry Love.

To you my answers probably sound like most other murder cases. The old love-hate combine again.

Go on.

Even if it's a cliché?

Even so.

Okay, I love *Trade or Betrayed*. I think it's the greatest enter-tainment of the twentieth century.

Go on.

I won't say more now, at least not about the aesthetics of the show—but in the sheer brilliance of concept it rivals the subtlety and simplicity of science. Think of its elements. Tina Rodriguez, the first important character since Harpo Marx who does not speak on screen. She has no horn, only silky thighs and a magic hand that points to a box wherein lies some housewife's dream. Tina herself has the shiny beauty of a major appliance. A night with her would clean your clothes, freeze and cook your meals, compact your trash. She is the end of all process, the statue of property in front of those big stars-and-stripes boxes. Meanwhile Larry is out in the audience forming the equation to which she is the answer.

I've seen the show. I know how it works. People dress up and make fools of themselves.

That's what I used to think. I used to think it was their own fault. People have always been making fools of themselves. Think of *Beat the Clock* or *Stop the Music*. And what about *Truth or Consequences*? Bob Barker has grown into an eccentric millionaire getting ladies' clubs from Burbank to eat crow for a twenty-five-dollar gift certificate from the Spiegel catalogue. I've never made an attempt on his life. Dennis James, Bill Cullen, Allen Ludden, I have no animosities for other daytime TV people. They're okay with me, a relief from the soap operas. But with Larry it was different. Sure the prizes are the stars, while the people dressed up as club sandwiches and cartoon characters hopping and popping at the chance to win something—the people are subhuman. Okay, so far I've said only what every reasonable person probably thinks when he first watches the show. I said it to people too. I thought it was camp that I liked *Trade or Betrayed*. I was wrong. After several years of watching, I realized that Larry is not kidding. He appears daily like the sun to remind you what the world is. Larry is the culmination of television. He teases you like Art Linkletter (who is another one I'd get if CBS hadn't cut him), but Larry is oh so sweet when he wants to be, giving comfort like the late Hal March consoling a $32,000 loser into a Cadillac. Ted Mack was the purest of the bunch. Every ragtag piece of talent wanted thirty seconds of playing a musical comb or twirling a baton while the wheel of fortune spun like Ted Mack's tongue spooning down the Geritol. What they did mattered not. The show came on at four p.m. on Sunday. But Larry slips in at the meridian promising electric comforts if you exploit your greed. He heats you for an afternoon of shopping. ·I found his statistics once in *TV Guide* and sent them under my name to an astrologer in Minneapolis. Do you know who Larry resembles most on the list of the five hundred most famous men in history?

I haven't any idea.

Abe Lincoln. And the match is identical. How's that for irony. Honest Abe and Slippery Larry, the two faces of a coin. The implications are immense. It affirmed my faith in astrology.

But what about your reasons for the murder?

Isn't the slightest bit of it becoming clear?

I'm sorry, but I don't follow you.

Get thee behind me, Satan. . . .

Please try to be less cryptic.

Did you get that on the tape?

Yes, it's a sixty-minute tape, you'll hear it end, so don't worry.

I hadn't stopped, counselor, I only paused for dramatic effect. When I recognized that Larry was Satan, I decided to kill him. The act was a straightforward moral choice. I had a clear and distinct knowledge of his evil and I decided to do something about it.

And you expect to present that as your defense? A jury won't even have time for coffee before they put you away for life.

Are all lawyers like this, or am I cursed with a bottom-of-the-class special?

Mr. Cook, I told you that I can resign at any time. I don't have to take any abuse from you, and if you don't speed up your statement I'm going to leave, abuse or no abuse.

Okay, Mr. Law and Order, I can see that you really don't want the whole story, only the blood and the guts. How it happened and then good-bye and good luck. You're the Joe Friday type, only the facts, ma'am, stiff-lipped anal personality. Okay, I'll give it to you like it was. I'll save the best stuff for the court, where you'll sit with hands in your pockets because you had no patience with me before the trial. You won't have a thing to say to the newsmen crowded around the door of the courtroom. They'll think its only legal aplomb. You won't be unique. A lot of stupidity passes for style. Not Larry, though, that was one smart son of a bitch. I'll never take that away from him.

How did you get into the audience?

Like everyone else. I waited a year for tickets, dressed up, and stood in line on La Cienega Boulevard.

How were you dressed?

You know that's one thing I don't like to talk about.

If I were a psychiatrist I might ask why, but as a lawyer I only want to know if your costume had anything at all to do with the murder.

Only in the sense that my own folly enraged me and I had a headache from the fruit. All right, I'll tell you—it's not that important. I came dressed as a basket of fruit. All over myself I hung plums, apricots, bing cherries. I wore grapes as ankle bracelets and a necklace of pumpkin seeds and artichoke leaves. On all parts of my chest, the berries hung from me at the end of strips of surgical tape. Hollowed out cantaloupes were my kneepads. On my head was a wide-brimmed straw hat with about two pounds of apples and pears glued on. I carried a vinyl inner-tube cushion, the kind hemorrhoid patients use, so I wouldn't squash the fruit against my legs. I went to all this trouble because I wanted to be sure he would notice me. Snug in my pocket lay a Browning automatic for which I paid three times the price of the Italian rifle that got John Kennedy.

Larry was good that day. He and Mike Fields did the audience warm-up themselves, telling salesman jokes and teasing Tina Rodriguez, who stayed spectral on the stage, moving like Tinkerbell between the stoves and refrigerators that stagehands were sliding behind Japanese screens. I had an aisle seat in the third row. I knew there was better than a fifty-fifty chance that he'd pick me. My sign said "Cornucopia." I knew that he wouldn't be able to resist making a joke about "corny" and "cornucopia," then he would ask me why I didn't have any corn. It happened precisely as I had anticipated it, and this too reinforced my belief that I was acting a destined role, that all my judgments were correct.

But the wait, the wait was unbearable. The murder was a breather compared to that. I am tall as you can see, and wearing that high hat and sitting on the vinyl inner tube made me even more conspicuous. The woman on my left was one of those screaming nymphomaniacs Larry always culls out. She was dressed as a safety match. "I'd like to strike up a trade," her sign coyly stated. From neck to knees she read "Ohio Blue Tip." "I really am from Columbus," she said. She kept threatening to eat my fruit. "I didn't have breakfast or lunch. I couldn't keep a thing down, I was so nervous about all this. Now I just want to eat your hat." She also deserved killing, but my eyes stayed on his sharkskin suit gliding up and down the stairs, while he searched his pockets for the right envelopes. "Now, we're going to use Larry's money machine, right, Fred? For the second gimmick, okay. Then Mike will come down with the box. Be sure you flash a card on that so I won't forget."

He pretended not to notice me during the warm-up while he teased a pair of twins from Mississippi who came as a fire hydrant and a dog. Their mother sat in the nonparticipants section and broke out in broad southern, "Give it to 'em, sisters, give it to 'em." She thought they were already on the air and urged her daughters, "The box, the box." Mike calmed her down. The audience loved it, but I could see Larry decide on the spot not to use them. Little did he know what lay quietly hidden in my cornucopia. The match pounced up and down whenever he faced us, but Larry was slick, playing to the sides, to the people who have no real chance of getting on the show. He used them to break the ice while those of us in the middle sat sweating in the studio lights. I watched Tina and desired her from afar. About ten minutes before air time he left us with Mike and an assistant director who wanted to make sure we all watched the applause sign.

"If Larry picks you, just do what he tells you. And remember, this is a half-hour show. If you stall too long on your choices, Larry can disqualify you. It's happened before. All winners come backstage afterwards to fill out IRS and delivery forms. We want you to have fun. Hold up your signs when Mike says, 'And here's America's number-one trader, Larry Love,' and then put them on the floor unless Larry asks for yours."

He was a wretched man the assistant director. Pale as an onion, he looked as if Larry kept him in a shaded cage except for this brief daily performance.

The red lights flashed all around. My sign was in the air. Larry strutted down the aisle in the light blue suit and the witch next to me pulled a German prune off my chest. "I can't wait, I'll faint." She ate noisily and I hoped she would choke on the pit.

Larry had everything, style, wit, charm, generosity, and hundreds of dollars in his pockets. For his opening bit he pretended to light a corncob pipe that he took from an old man at the back of the room.

"I haven't got a match, let's see, should I use this?" He pulled a five hundred dollar bill from his pocket. "No," we moaned in unison. Hands clutched toward the aisle as if they were saving a drowning child.

"Okay then, I won't smoke. I'll give this money to Irene Henderson, right here." Larry played her like an instrument. She was a buxom negress from Pennsylvania dressed as an angel. She was two rows behind me, but when she flapped her big arms to show Larry how angels fly, she splattered me with a combination of sweat and fluffy goose down coming loose from her wings. Larry got her to try to fly, then he allowed her time to tug at her big afro while she tried to decide whether to keep the five hundred or go for the box, a big American flag guarded by Tina Rodriguez in pale green shorts and a halter. Tina's soft hand opened to the box as if she were introducing a foreign dignitary. The black woman moaned and tried to locate her husband somewhere deep in the audience.

"I'll keep the money," she screamed. Tina waved her magic hand, the flag-box slid away revealing a Speed Queen washer-dryer, a six-hundred-dollar number. "But still a very good deal for Irene Henderson, who has herself five hundred dollars, right, little angel?" Larry leaves her squeezing bills. He monkeys around with three people and a purse, then he has newlyweds guess the prices of a series of items: popcorn, olives, shaving cream, and an electric saw. The couple misses everything by a mile, ruining his chance to give away a car. Larry gives them fifty dollars to go to a supermarket and learn something about prices. You can see the anger in his eyes; the newlyweds have cost him the highlight of the show, the suspense over a car. America needs a big number now. I am facing forward, stony, ice in my veins, but I know he comes by the match popping up and down beside me. "Me," she is saying with private sincerity, "please, God, let him pick me." Over and over her prayer in my ear as Larry pauses at our row, checking the match, a pound cake, a bottle of champagne, and then me, his destiny in the sweet garb of nature. I tower over him as he reads my name tag. My head is pounding from the weight of the hat. He tells me to take it off so he can see my face. He looks into my eyes the way Ken and Edith must have gazed at one another in that Rexall store in Elmira. I have the momentary impression that he is clairvoyant, that he knows me and fears me not. He puts his arm around me and offers a choice, the box Tina is standing in front of on the stage or the one Mike is bringing down the aisle toward us. Tina has changed into a red velvet gown that brushes against the box, ten feet tall and covered in aluminum foil. The lights glare off it and off the pale skin of Tina. "The big box," says the match, "the big box," in her prayerful tone. Larry has made the predicted joke about corn and cornucopia. I pretend to fidget with my belt while I bring out that gleaming beauty, my Browning automatic.

"Larry," I say, "there is no choice and we both know it." The moment has come. Without a gasp the audience disappears into silence. Mike crawls under his box, which contains, I suppose, a tea service from the Michael C. Fina Company. The assistant director starts up the aisle but stops and then retreats when I put the Browning squarely at Larry's Brylcreemed temple. Larry is preternaturally calm, as if there is only a washing machine at stake. "Go ahead if you must," he says, "in this business time is money." The last impulse I have toward him is one of admiration, the kind of admiration you have for something so wholly conceived that its essential nature is untouched by experience. Larry is encased like a zoological specimen. In that last instant I see that he is more eternal than my desire to destroy him. My finger twitches at the Browning, my resolution wavers. From the stage, for the first time in her silent decade, comes the voice of Tina, more passionate than her velvet gown. "Shoot," she calls out as I caress the trigger until Larry's head seems but an extension of my arm. A second time comes her voice clear as a cathedral organ, "Shoot." From under the box where he had sought refuge, Mike Fields implores me no less richly than Tina, "Shoot quickly." The silent audience picks up the cadence. They yell for me to shoot just the way they called out "the money" or "the box" earlier. Larry flashes his white teeth. On a steady palm he blows a soft kiss in the direction of Tina. To me he forms "shoot" with his lips as if he's cheating at charades, and holding him tight as a lover, I do. I hear the Browning hit the floor before Larry does. He falls first to his knees, his head against my arm so that I feel his teeth scrape my life line. I move back and he goes down hard, his last sound the magnified scratching of his starched shirt against the microphone.

I must have gone into shock immediately after it happened because I don't remember anything until I was outside on La Cienega Boulevard pulling the fruit off my body. The surgical tape stung and the sun almost knocked me over. It felt like that gaudy noon heat just sat on me. For shade I crouched under the awning of a bookstore. There were no customers, only paperbacks being watched by a security camera. My breath fogged the window. I tried to go in for the air conditioning but the door was locked. I must have been outside only a few minutes, but I felt like I was locked into one of those portable steam cabinets where your head sticks out like a vegetable and the rest of you shrinks away in the hiss. I choked against the window but nobody noticed me. A tourist bus coming into the ABC lot almost knocked me over. The driver's horn was still in my ear as I returned to the *Trade or Betrayed* set. Yes, I came back, just like the saying. It took Raskolnikov hundreds of pages to return, I did it in less than a block. As soon as I opened the heavy studio door I felt much better. A studio policeman shoved me against the back wall. "No talking," he said, "we're still on the air."

Mike Fields, holding Larry's microphone, stood between Irene

Henderson and the Ohio Blue Tip, who were competing for the big trade of the day. The black angel pecked kisses at Mike as if she were drilling his teeth. On stage, Tina waved her thighs at two hundred dollars' worth of Masland carpeting. Larry himself lay compact in the aisle, a small bundle near my vacated seat. His patent shoes gleamed. The din of competition did not affect me as I concentrated on Larry's Lincolnesque silhouette shaded in dark ooze like the trickle from beneath a refrigerator. The organ picked up the *Trade or Betrayed* theme and we faded, he and I now completed, into one p.m. and *The Newlywed Game.*

Patty-Cake, Patty-Cake... A Memoir

I

When he took walks, G.R. hummed "Cruising down the River." Now and then he munched on red pistachio nuts and spit the shells over the curb. I had to trot to keep up with his long steps. Once we got to the bakery, he'd go donut wild. Cream puffs, eclairs, even the cherryfilled Danish were nothing to him. He headed for the plain brown donuts, what my father called fry cakes. He ate each one in two bites, coming down exactly in the middle of the hole everytime. Daddy would give him a couple dozen like nothing. Everybody on Franklin Street gave things to G.R. There wasn't a housewife who didn't feel proud to fry him a few donuts herself. And why the hell not? He raked their leaves, carried groceries, opened doors, and smiled at the old folks. He was an Eagle Scout. I was just his nigger sidekick but people liked me for being that. Much later I got good jobs, loans, even my own business because of being his sidekick. But when we started, it was G.R. that needed me. He used to think my old man gave him the donuts because he was my buddy. He didn't know for a long time how much people liked him.

"Christ," I used to tell him, "Daddy would give you fry cakes even if you stomped me once a week. He likes you, G.R. You're his neighbor."

In fact we were sort of double neighbors. Our houses were on the same block and his father's paint store was just down the street from the American Bakery, where my dad was the donut and cake man.

G.R. and I hung around the Bridge Street branch of the public library. He read the sports books and I did the science fiction. Then we'd go to the bakery and he'd start to wolf down the fry cakes. He ate all he could, then stuffed his pockets. My old man just used to laugh and throw in a few more. A dozen was a light snack to him. After football games, he always had his twelve fresh ones waiting in the locker room. He never shared, although he was generous with everything else. He ate them with his cleats and helmet still on and sometimes mud all over his face.

When my father died, G.R. and I were in college. He came over to the Alpha Kappa Psi house, hugged me, and said, "Sonny, you know how he did it, you've got to take over." And like a dumb ass, I did. I made them at night in the big Alpha Kappa Psi deep fryer. But G.R. always paid for the ingredients.

You've got to remember that this was 1937 and he was the social chairman of the DU's, the best of the white houses, and a big football player, and I was still his nigger sidekick from home to everyone except the brothers of Alpha Kappa Psi, where I was the house treasurer.

It only took about an hour once a week or so, and he liked them so much that I just couldn't stop. It would have been like weaning a baby. I didn't want to put up with all his moping. G.R. wasn't unhappy much, but when he was, the whole DU house could burn up and he wouldn't leave his room. I was the only one he let in. He'd sit and stare at a 12 × 5 of his father and mother in front of the paint store. He'd say things like, "Sonny, they did a lot for me and no goddamn girl is going to ruin it." Or if it wasn't a girl, it was a goddamn professor or sometimes a goddamn coach.

After a mope he'd be good for two dozen and a half gallon of milk. The brothers used to call me his mammy. "The big old ballplayer needs mammy's short'nin' bread," they used to say when they'd see me starting up the deep fryer after an emergency call from someone at DU. That's why half the house called me mammy, even though my actual nickname was Sonny. In the

Michigan Ensign for 1938, there I am in the group picture of the only black frat house in Ann Arbor. "Sonny 'Mammy' Williams," it says, "Treasurer." G.R. is all over the book with the DU's, the football team, the Audubon Society, the Student Union, the Intrafraternity Honor Council. I counted him eight times and who knows how many I missed.

I think the only reason I ever went to Ann Arbor instead of JC like my sisters was that he was going and he got me a piece of his scholarship somehow. But when he went to law school, I said, "No dice, ace, I'm not hauling my ass up to Harvard." And I got a job back in Grand Rapids working for Rasberry Heating. Law School was the first time he got by without the fry cakes and he said he was a grump all three years.

"I lost seventeen pounds and almost married a girl I didn't love," he told me when he came back. "I lost a lot of my judgment and some of my quickness. Harvard and Yale may have class, Sonny, but when you come down to it, there's no place like home." He came back from Harvard as patriotic as the soldiers shipping back from Guam a few years later. I met him at the Market Street station with a sign that said, "Welcome back, Counselor," and a dozen hot fry cakes. His Ma and Dad were there too and his brother Phil. He hugged us all, ate the donuts, and said, "If you seek a beautiful peninsula, look around you." Then he said it in Latin and we thought it was lawyer's talk and we looked the train station over real good. Then he told us it was the motto of the state of Michigan, which was founded in 1837 and was the first state west of Pennsylvania to have its own printing press. He said he wasn't leaving Michigan for a good long time, and if it wasn't for the war a few months later, I don't believe he would have.

The war started in December and he came back from Harvard in the June before that. The first thing he did was make me take my two weeks from Rasberry and head up to the Upper Peninsula with him. "To the thumb, Sonny, to the tip of Michigan where three great lakes sparkle and iron and copper dot the landscape."

I still couldn't say no to the guy so I went along even though

I knew the Upper Peninsula was for Indians and not for Negroes.

We drove two days in my '35 Chevy, up through Cadillac, Reed City, Petoskey, Cheboygan. The roads were bad. When we had a flat near the Iron River, it took an hour for another car to come by so we could borrow a jack. I wished all the time that we were on our way to Chicago or Cleveland or Indianapolis or someplace where you could do something when you got there. But old G.R. was on a nature kick then. I believe Harvard and no fry cakes had about driven him nuts. While I flagged down the jack, he stood beside the car and did deep knee bends and Marine push-ups. He took off his shirt and beat his chest. "Smell the air, Sonny, that's Michigan for you," he said. People were suspicious enough about stopping for a nigger trying to flag them down without this bouncing Tarzan to scare 'em worse.

When we finally got the ferryboat to take us to Mackinac Island, I knew it was a mistake. The only negroes besides me were the shoeshine boys on the boat, and here I was in a linen suit and big straw hat alongside Mr. Michigan, who was taking in the Lake Superior spray and still beating his chest now and then and telling everyone what a treat it was to live in the Thumb state. Everybody thought I was his valet, so when I caught some real bad staring I just went over and brushed his jacket or something and the folks smiled at me very nicely. I didn't want trouble then and I don't now. I've been a negro all my life and no matter how hard I try I can't call myself a black.

Another thing I tell people and they can hardly believe is that I don't think G.R. ever once said anything about my color. I don't believe he ever noticed it or thought about it or considered that it made a bit of difference. I guess that's another reason why I didn't mind baking his donuts.

But Mackinac Island was a mistake for both of us. I was bored stiff by talking about how good the food was in the hotel and taking little rides in horse-drawn carriages. G.R. seemed to like it, so I didn't say much.

One morning he says, "Sonny, let's get clipped," and I go with him to the hotel barbershop without giving it a thought. After being there a week, I must have lost my sense, too, to just go along like that. He sits down in one vacant chair and motions me to the other. There are a couple of thin barbers who look like their scissors. I'm just getting my socks adjusted and looking down at "Theo A. Kochs" written on the bottom of the barber chair when my thin man says almost in a whisper, "I'm sorry, sir, but we don't do negro hair." G.R. hasn't heard this because his barber has snapped the striped sheet loudly around him and is already combing those straight blond strands.

I step out of the chair. "No hard feelings," he says.

"None," I say, "I didn't need a haircut anyway. I'll just wait for my friend here."

"Fine," he says, and sits down in his chair to have a smoke while he waits for another customer.

When G.R. gets turned around and sees this little barber lighting up, he says, "Sonny, c'mon, I thought we're both getting clipped this morning."

"I'll wait, G.R.," I say, hoping he'll let it go.

"No waiting," he says. "It's sharp country up here, we've got to look sharp for it, right, boys?" He looks at my little barber who blows some smoke and says, "I'm sorry, but we don't cut colored hair here. In fact, I don't think there's a spot on the island that does. We just don't get that much in colored trade."

"What do you mean you don't cut colored hair?" G.R. says.

"Just what I said." The barber is a little nervous. He stands up and starts to wash some combs, but G.R. is out of his chair now and facing him against a row of mirrors.

"What do you mean by colored?" he asks the barber.

My barber looks at his partner. I am getting pissed at G.R. for making something out of this. I should have known better. At home I wouldn't just walk into the Pantlind or the Rowe Hotel and expect to get a haircut.

"It's okay, G.R.," I say. "Sit down and let's get going. We've got lots to see yet, Indian villages and copper mines and remnants of old beaver trappers' lodges."

"I want to know what this man means by colored," he says, crowding the little barber against a display of Wildroot Cream Oil. The other barber, G.R.'s, says, "Look, mister, why don't the both of you just take your business someplace else." G.R. is a very big man and both barbers together don't weigh two fifty. He says it again. "I want to know what this man means by colored." He is trailing them in the white cover sheet with black stripes and a little paper dickey around his neck. He looks like Lou Gehrig in a Yankee nightshirt. My barber is afraid to say anything but the other one says, "Well, look at your friend's teeth real white, see, and the palms of his hands are brownish pink, and his hair is real woolly. I couldn't pull that comb I just used on you through that woolly hair now, could I?" G.R. looks surprised.

"And when you've got white teeth and pinky brown palms and woolly hair and your skin is either black or brown, then most people call you colored. You understand now?"

"But what's that got to do with haircuts?" G.R. asks. Nobody knows what to say now. The barbers don't understand him, so I step up and say, "They need special instruments to cut my hair, G.R. It's like he says, those puny little combs don't go through this, see. I got to go to my own kind of barber so he'll know how to handle me."

G.R. was edgy all through his haircut and he didn't leave a tip, but once we left the barbershop I believe he forgot the whole thing.

But the way he was with those barbers, that's how he operated with girls too. What I mean is, he didn't understand what they were getting at. And this was a shame because he really attracted the ladies. They didn't all come at him like ducks to popcorn, but if he stayed at a school dance for an hour or so, the prettiest girl there would be over talking to him and joking and maybe even dancing with him. He never did anything but talk and joke them. He'd walk home with me. I'd say, "G.R., that Peggy Blanton was giving you the eye. Why'd you pass up something like that?"

"Training," he'd say, or "Hell, Sonny, I came to the dance with you and I'm leaving with you." If there'd ever been a good-looking colored girl there I sure wouldn't have left with him. Don't get me wrong, G.R. was a regular man, nothing the matter with his glands; he just wasn't as interested in girls as most of us were. One weekend in college he drove to Chicago with me and some of the brothers of Alpha Kappa Psi. The brothers wanted some of that good jazz from down around Jackson Avenue and G.R. wanted to see the White Sox play baseball. He took a bus to Comiskey Park for a doubleheader and met us about eight at the Blue Box, where those great colored jazz groups used to be in those days. G.R. stood out like a light bulb. We'd been there all afternoon just mellow and strung out on the music. G.R. came in and wanted to talk baseball. Don't forget that in those days the White Sox really were white and the brothers could have cared less what a group of whites were doing that afternoon up on Lake Shore Drive.

"You should have seen Luke Appling," he was saying; "there's not a man in either league who can play that kind of shortstop." Nobody paid any attention to G.R. He didn't drink and the music was just noise to him. He had taken a book along and was trying to read in the candlelight at the Blue Box. You had to feel sorry for him. It was so dark in there you couldn't see your fingers at arm's length. The atmosphere was heavy with music, liquor, women. I mean the place was cool, relaxed, nobody doing more than tapping a glass, and he sits there squinting over a big blue book, underlining things and scratching his head like he's in the library. He was alone at a table so he could concentrate, but I kept my eye on him just in case anything came up. Pretty soon two really smooth numbers come over to his table. Now you'd call them "Foxes." They were in evening gowns and very loose, maybe even drunk. He was the only white man in the place and they kind of giggled at him and sat down. I couldn't hear a word they said but I watched every move. I could see because they'd started using a spotlight for the small stage and G.R. was a little to one side of it.

One of the girls starts rubbing the spine of the blue book. The other one takes his finger and puts it on the page. She uses his hand like a big pointer. Maybe she's asking him what some of those big words mean. They're both real close. I start to get a little jealous. I've been there all day with nothing like that kind of action. But, it's like I said, he had a way with the girls. They seem to be talking a lot. The girls are real dreamy on him, one under each arm. It looks like he's reading out loud to them because one of them is holding the book up for him to read from. Whatever he's reading is really breaking the girls up. One of them is kind of tickling his belly with a fingernail between the buttons of his shirt. Sam Conquest and his combo were doing a set then that really had us going. I mean, as much as I was keeping an eye out for G.R., I was into the music too and couldn't really be sure about what my buddy was getting himself into. All I know is that I slipped into the music for just a couple of minutes and when I looked back he was gone. So were the girls and his book. What the hell, I thought, anyone else would, why not G.R. too?

It wasn't until we got back to Ann Arbor and were alone together in his room that G.R. told me what really happened with those two girls.

"I was robbed," he said. "They got about four dollars, but it was all I had. I think Shirlene did it." He showed me his finger with a Band-Aid on it. "I cut myself on the sequins of her dress. She was giving me kind of a chest rub and my arm was around her. I thought she really liked me, Sonny. I cut my finger real deep on one of those sequins. Doris went to the drugstore for a Band-Aid. While she was gone, I think Shirlene got her hand into my trousers and took the four bucks. I was telling them about World War I. They were interested in Woodrow Wilson and the League of Nations. I don't know why they robbed me. If she would have asked me, I'd have given her the four dollars, you know I would have, don't you, Sonny?"

"G.R.," I said, smiling but real sad about him, "you good-looking DU social chairman, you football captain and White Sox fan, what the hell is ever going to happen to you in the real world? You can't tell robbery from love, you don't have the ear for music or the eye for color. You can eat donuts and tackle people, you're a good citizen. Get tough, get mean, drink whiskey, swear, slap some chicks around, fuck a few, stop saying yes ma'am, turn in your homework late, cut football practice, cheat on exams, wear dirty socks ... I mean, Jesus Christ, be like everybody else." I broke down then. I liked him so much the way he was that it killed me to say these things, but I did it for his sake. Somebody had to warn him.

He put his arm around me while I sobbed. "Sonny," he said, "I'll try."

II

When he ran for Congress he laid off the fry cakes. By then, with his help in getting me a loan, guess who owned the American Bakery? He was making good money as a lawyer. I thought he was crazy to run for the Congress. When I heard it on the radio, I brought a dozen fry cakes fresh from the oven right up to his office in the Federal Square Building. He had a little refrigerator where he kept his milk and his lunch. I hadn't even taken off my white baker's outfit. Some court photographer happened to be in the building and snapped a picture of me in whites carrying the donuts and looking mad as hell. Right after he became the President, *The New York Times* printed that picture and I started getting flooded with requests from TV. That's when the President's baker thing got started. I sold the American Bakery in '58 and have hardly dipped a fry cake since then, but once a story gets on TV you're stuck with it. Never mind that I'm in auto leasing and sporting goods now; the "President's baker" is what I'm destined to remain.

But the day of that picture was an important one: it was the last day of our real friendship. I slipped past a secretary and gave him the dozen. His desk was full of papers. "Later," he said. "Right now," I told him, and I stood there waiting. He was always more sensible after donuts and milk. I went right to his refrigerator and brought out the bottle of Sealtest. I stood there until he was done. "G.R.," I said, "why the hell are you doing this? Aren't you the man who told me you'd never leave Michigan? You've got your friends here and your family, what's all this about going to Washington, D.C.? If you want politics, what about being mayor?"

"Sonny, there's a big country out there and most of it is full of Democrats. And there's untold Communists around the world just waiting to get their fingers on your bakery and my law office and everything else we've been working for."

"G.R.," I said, "if you leave this town you're making the mistake of your life."

He looked up at me from his desk. "Sonny, if you're not for me you're against me."

"Get your fry cakes in D.C.," I told him, "and your friends too." I walked out. I voted against him that time and in every other election, and as far as I know he never again tasted one of my donuts. He moved to D.C. that January. Every year I get a Christmas card and a district newsletter, but until he became President that was it. Not even a phone call when he was in town. What the hell, I thought to myself, he turned his back on his old friends but I guess it's what he really wanted. He spent twenty-five years in D.C. without me and without those donuts and he didn't seem to miss Michigan all that much either. I, who was his nigger sidekick and his college "mammy," never saw his wife or his kids. When his dad died I went to the funeral, but the crowd was so big I didn't even get into the chapel. At the cemetery it was private. I thought I saw G.R. in one of the limousines while they were loading the casket in, but you can't run up and talk to a man at a time like that. Yessir, G.R. and I were through, cold turkey, until that night last August when Nixon resigned.

To tell you the truth, until the minute it happened none of us believed Nixon would ever be out of there until '76. When they interrupted the Tigers game with the news, you could have knocked me over with a feather. People all over town started walking around the streets like they were drunk. The JCCs painted a big Home of the President poster and had it up at the northern city limits within an hour. My mother, who's in a home now, called up to remind me that she taught the President how to tie his shoes. He was fast, Mama remembered, and double knotted every time. And the truth is, although I had resented him being a Congressman all those years, I spent a few minutes just saying out loud, "G.R., Mr. President." I said it over and over. I was still saying it when I got a phoned-in telegram from his press secretary. "Sonny—Emergency. Air Force One will pick you up midnight Grand Rapids airport." It was signed G.R. A White House operator read it to me at ten o'clock while I was watching the newsmen do a wrap-up on Nixon. He wasn't officially President until the next day but already he could send Air Force One out to do his errands.

I knew what this meant. I packed a blue suit and my own deep fryer, and it's a good thing I did. With all the stuff in that White House kitchen, there isn't a single deep fryer. I heard one of the cooks grumbling that Jackie Kennedy had it thrown away and Johnson used to eat all his fries on the ranch. Nixon only cared for pan-fried. The cooks were mighty suspicious. Here was the new President who they didn't even know sending over his own old boy with a personal deep fryer.

I was met at the airport by a nice young fellow. He took my grocery order. The Presidential limousine waited outside the all-night Safeway while we shopped. I overbought, made twelve dozen because for all I knew he wanted to treat the whole cabinet. By seven on the morning of the day he was to become the President, G.R. had his fry cakes, crisp on the outside, soft on the inside. I was a little nervous in case I'd lost my touch but this was one sweet batch. An FBI man delivered all twelve dozen. The White House cooks treated me very uppity. They were all tears about Nixon, wondering whether he could stomach bacon and eggs for his last breakfast, and here I was whipping out twelve dozen donuts for the new boy. They didn't know if they could keep up with an appetite like that.

I hung around the kitchen because I didn't know where else to go. You wouldn't believe the chaos. Nixon sent back the coffee, bacon, and eggs. He was going to be on TV at ten. They sent up cream of wheat, rye toast, coffee, and vegetable juice. It came back too. The juice glass was empty but there were lipstick stains on it.

"The poor man hasn't moved his bowels yet," the cook said when he saw Nixon giving his last speech. "Without morning coffee, he is cement. He hasn't slept either. Oh God, what's going to happen to all of us?" He looked at me and then spit into the sink. We were crowded together watching a twelve-inch Sony color set.

I had a late breakfast with the kitchen staff and hung around the TV for G.R.'s swearing-in and his speech. I played some gin rummy with a few maids. Limousines kept pulling up outside but the whole place was quiet as a white funeral parlor. Just before noon that same young man who met my plane came into the kitchen and gave me an envelope. There was a regular Central Air Lines ticket in it, but for first class, a hundred dollar bill, and a note. The note said, "Just like old times. Thanks, G.R."

I watched him on TV with Nixon's kitchen help. They were all zombies by noon. One of them said he dreamed that Nixon changed his mind in the air and was going to phone in at eleven fifty-nine to say hold off that swearing-in. I was the only one blindly excited and proud. And I don't have to tell you that my man was cool as a cucumber and straight as an arrow. There were some snickers in the kitchen when the camera showed General Haig brushing some crumbs off the new President's lapel. I saw them in color, the yellow crumbs I knew. "Here fellas," I said, tossing the hundred in the air, "have a drink on your new boss."

I was home by nightfall and haven't heard from him since. I guess that he's trying to make a go of it with that bunch of cooks he inherited. Still, who knows G.R. like I do? When it gets really tough in that oval office he'll start to smell the fry cakes. When that happens, watch out Kissinger and the Joint Chiefs. Mr. Donut and Dixie Cream won't be enough. His lips will start to twitch and his teeth will bite the air. He'll remember the glorious peninsula and the three Great Lakes of the Thumb. His mouth will water for the real thing. And when that happens, in the pinch, The President knows old Sonny won't let him down.